GRYPHON OF GLASS

ZOE CHANT

For Layla, for making the impossible possible.

CONTENTS

FAE SHIFTER KNIGHTS

This book does stand alone, with a satisfying happy ever after, but it is part of a series that will be most enjoyed in order:

Dragon of Glass (book 1)
Unicorn of Glass (book 2)
Gryphon of Glass (book 3)
Firebird of Glass (forthcoming!)

*D*ing dong!

The doorbell sent Trey and Rez scrambling for the knob, trying good-naturedly to knock each other aside with their elbows. They flung the door open so vigorously that the children outside drew back in surprise before screaming "Trick or treat!" at the top of their little lungs.

The kids were dressed in an assortment of costumes: a princess carrying a sword and wearing a wool cap in deference to the chilly air, a blue furry monster swiveling its head to see out of tiny eye holes, a mermaid with a sequined tail over her arm, two superheroes, and a knight.

"A tiny fellow knight!" Trey exclaimed in delight, and he and Rez both bowed respectfully.

The child knight looked like he was trying to decide if they were making fun of him.

"I'm Iron Man!" one of the other costumed children declared. The mermaid tried to hide behind her tail.

The two parties stood staring at each other until the blue monster asked, "Where's the candy?" in a muffled voice.

Gwen, leaning just inside the door, held the bowl out to Trey and Rez with a grin. They took fistfuls of candy and emptied them into the offered bags and plastic pumpkins.

"Truly, I thought you were jesting," Rez said, as the children tramped happily away down the walkway back to the quiet street. The unicorn shifter shook his head in wonder.

"It is a most puzzling custom," Trey agreed.

"Are you sure that adults cannot also do this?" Rez asked wistfully, watching the kids comparing treats as they returned to their trek down the street.

"It's the greatest tragedy of growing up," Gwen said mournfully. "We're going to need more candy at this rate! Where did it all *go?*"

Trey looked guilty. "The tiny sweets were very tempting."

"I picked up another bag while I was out yesterday," Ansel called from the kitchen. "Thank you, Ansel!" he joked.

"You're an angel, Ansel!" Gwen hollered back.

"No, you're the angel!"

Gwen was dressed in a flimsy white dress over leggings, a halo on her head and tiny pair of feathered wings held on with elastic.

"Beg to differ," Gwen retorted.

Ansel worked some kind of highly variably technical computer job remotely, occasionally taking long business trips to consult. The second hand store that he owned in Wimberlette was clearly not something he required for solvency but seemed to be something he used as a way of emptying a cluttered old house that he'd inherited. Instead of complaining when a dragon broke a hole in the roof of his shop to fight horrible dark forces from another world and trashed his warehouse, he had offered a room in his home to Gwen, who had come through a portal from across the country without a wallet in her pocket and no way to get home. Heather and her unicorn-shifting fae knight, Rez, had followed from Georgia several months later. Daniella and Trey (who happened to be the dragon that had clawed through his shop roof) spent so much time at Ansel's house that he finally suggested that they simply move in and save on rent.

He only asked that they keep the space clean and the fridge stocked, and calmly converted half of his gigantic garage into a sparring space.

Rez and Trey stood watching out of the window while Gwen took the bowl in to refill. "Another troop approaches!" Trey announced with great excitement.

Ansel and Gwen exchanged an amused look and Gwen hurried back to the living room with the coveted candy.

The knights greeted this group with a little more decorum and happily handed out brightly-decorated candy to the squealing kids wearing an array of handmade and store-bought costumes.

The next group was already scrambling up the stairs before the last ones were gone, and for a short while, the knights were kept busy filling pillowcases and tote bags.

"It is so delightful here," Rez said, looking wistfully after the children. "So safe and happy."

"Pray we keep it thus," Trey said mournfully. The dragon shifter slung a casual arm around his shieldmate.

Gwen watched them exchange a look of sorrow and played with her sparkly tinsel halo.

Sometimes it was hard to remember the impending danger. The boundary between her world and theirs would become weaker and weaker towards the end of the year, and when it was thinnest, the darkness that had destroyed their land would try to do the same here.

Gwen had already battled the forerunners of the attack, a terrible vicious *bleak* and the evil, mindless *dours* that it led.

What's more, she had seen the army they had tried to bring through at the last New Year's Eve and it still gave her nightmares, remembering how helpless she had been against them. She, Trey, Daniella, and Robin the fable had barely been able to turn them back, and Robin had suffered greatly to seal the portals that would have let them through.

Gwen re-settled her halo, regretting the fact that she hadn't been able to do much in the scope of things. Her sword was worthless against the shadowy form, slicing through it without doing any damage. Robin swore that she would come into her power once she was united with the gryphon-shifting knight, Henrik.

The only problem was that no one knew where Henrik might be.

Four of the knights had been captured in glass and thrust into a strange world with their mentor, Robin. These ornaments, a dragon, a unicorn, a gryphon, and a firebird, had been found by Ansel...and subsequently sold, one at a time.

Gwen sometimes wondered if his generosity was a matter of apology, for not recognizing the magical glass ornaments for what they were, and for accidentally separating the four of them. But Ansel's hospitality seemed genuine, and his appreciation for their situation was not feigned; if all four knights were not freed from their glass prisons and united with their keys, there would be little to stand between the dark forces of the place they'd come from and the helpless human world.

It seemed strange that their battle had been less than a year ago, and it was terrifying to think that they were no closer now to finding the two missing knights, with New Year's looming in a few short months.

A scream shook Gwen from her musing, and Trey and Rez both reached for the swords at their sides. Heather had decked them out in medieval costumes from her Renaissance Festival contacts, and they had real weapons from her blacksmith friend.

Gwen was the first one out the open door, but she knew before she got to the bottom of the porch steps that the scream was more outrage and surprise than pain.

A little brown-skinned boy was lying in the slushy snow beside the steps, holding his arm and wailing. His friends hovered over him in various states of scorn and sympathy.

"Hey there, Superman," Gwen said kindly, weaving between the kids. "Did you fall off the steps?"

"Jerry pushed me!" the little boy accused.

"I did not!" Jerry protested. "You slipped!"

"You going to want a bandaid on that?" Gwen asked, before they could argue about it further. "I bet we have some fun designs!"

The little boy brightened at the idea; he was wearing short sleeves despite the snow, and trying to crane to see his injured elbow. "Is it bleeding?"

"C'mon, I'll help you put it on," Gwen said. "The rest of you can come in and play with the dogs for a minute."

That brought them all tromping eagerly in with wet boots and laughter. Heather let Vesta down to greet them and Fabio bounded forward with his tail wagging the moment Daniella released his collar.

Vesta was a tiny Italian Greyhound, close in size to Gwen's cat Socks, who was undoubtedly hiding somewhere safe from dangerous doorbells and sticky, grabby fingers. Fabio was a full-sized Afghan Hound with a floating blond coat like the cover model he was named after. The children

were immediately enthralled with both of them, and the
boy holding his elbow looked like he wanted to stay and
play.

"I'm Gwen," she offered, herding the hurt superhero
into the kitchen. "What's your name?"

"Lawson," the little boy said sullenly. Gwen passed him
a piece of candy behind her back and he brightened
considerably.

"Looks like you got a little scrape," Gwen said casually
as he unwrapped the treat. "Let's clean it out and I'll find a
bandaid."

Lawson was inclined to snivel over the hydrogen
peroxide that Gwen used, but she easily distracted him.
"Did you know that I used to teach martial arts to kids just
your age?" she said.

"*You* know karate?" he asked skeptically.

"I'm a black belt in Tang Soo Do," Gwen said, adding,
"Fifth degree," even though it probably wouldn't mean
anything to him.

He looked duly impressed. "That's cool!"

She found a tube of antibiotic and squeezed out a tiny
bit to rub over the scratch, which had already stopped
bleeding.

"Feeling better?" Gwen asked.

Lawson shrugged, like he'd forgotten that there had
been any injury at all. "My mom has one of those!" he
said, pointing suddenly at the window.

"She has the same curtains?" Gwen asked, not looking.
She screwed the top back onto the antibiotic.

"The shiny glass ornaments," the small Batman
explained. "But ours is yellow. And a kitty-bird."

Gwen felt her breath catch in her throat, and she
nearly dropped the tube she was holding. He was
pointing at the two glass ornaments hanging from the

curtain rod, up out of the reach of two rambunctious dogs and an occasionally destructive cat. One was a green dragon in a ring of white, and one was a blue unicorn.

Those glass ornaments had once held Trey and Rez, imprisoned by magic.

"Like those?" Gwen said, choked. "Made of glass, with a white ring around it, and...it has wings?"

"Yeah! It's in the Christmas box. I'm not allowed to touch it. Do I get a bandaid?"

Gwen stared at Lawson for a long moment.

Henrik.

He had Henrik's ornament. Gwen felt a wave of surprise and near-panic break over her.

This was *it*. She really *was* going to get her knight...

...and everything that came with him. She was equal parts thrilled and afraid. She'd looked forward to this for so long.

"Are you okay? I want a bandaid."

Gwen shook herself. "Yeah, sure." Numbly, she fumbled the bandage box open and pulled one out. "We don't have anything cool," she apologized. "Just, er, beige."

It was pale on his mahogany-brown elbow, but Lawson looked pleased by the badge of honor anyway. "Thanks!"

When he would have sprung to his feet and rejoined his friends playing with the dogs in the front room, Gwen stopped him. "That ornament, it was part of a set, can I...uh...call your mom about it?"

"Sure!" Lawson said cheerfully and he would have left it at that if Gwen hadn't prodded him for a phone number, which he rattled off at full speed.

"Say it again," Gwen said desperately, reaching for pen and paper. "*Slower.*"

Releasing him back into the room with his friends and

the two self-declared love-starved dogs, Gwen stared at the number on the page.

Henrik.

Her...destiny?

Before she could lose her nerve, she picked up the house phone and dialed the number.

Only when the woman picked up did she realize that she hadn't asked for any names. "Is this Lawson's mom?" she asked hesitantly to the very young voice that answered.

"Hang on!"

After some garbled background conversation, someone crossly asked, "What?"

"Er, is this Lawson's mother?"

"What did he do?" she demanded.

"Nothing!" Gwen assured her quickly. "Nothing at all! Well, he fell down on our front step. I gave him a bandaid."

"He's okay?" the voice at the other end of the phone asked suspiciously.

"Fine," Gwen promised. "He screamed like a banshee, but forgot about it five minutes later."

She was rewarded with a chuckle. "Yeah, he does that. What's the problem? I need to come get him?"

Gwen paused. *I need your Christmas ornament to free a fae knight from another world* didn't seem like a successful way to start. *You have my destined fairy knight trapped in glass and I'd like him back, please* seemed, if anything, even crazier.

"I...ah...have a set of glass ornaments and it sounds like you have one of the pieces I'm missing. A golden gryphon in a white ring. A Christmas ornament. A...uh...kitty-bird." She wasn't doing a good job of not sounding weird.

Heather came swirling into the kitchen in her swishy Renaissance dress just then, oblivious to the fact that Gwen was on the phone. Vesta was tucked under her elbow and

Fabio was romping at her feet. "Hey Gwen—!" She lowered her voice considerably. "Sorry!"

At the other end of the line, Lawson's mother said off-handedly, "Yeah, I think we got that. Amberlynn, you leave your little sister alone right this moment!"

"Can I buy it from you?" Gwen blurted. "I'll pay whatever you want. It's...it's kind of important. Part of a set, you know." Should she say it was a family heirloom? Explain more?

Heather stared at her, mouthing a question, and Gwen had to turn away and listen closely over the poor connection and the sound of her own pounding heart. Fabio, unhelpfully, came prancing to greet her and lick her hand hopefully, his nails loud on the kitchen floor.

"I'm sorry, what was that?" she asked, when she couldn't make sense of the voice.

"Yeah, sure, I could part with it. I think I paid twenty for it."

"I could come get it right now!" Gwen said desperately, before she could stop herself.

"It's in storage," the woman said.

"Tomorrow?" Gwen said, trying to keep from sounding too eager. "Let me know your address, and I can swing by whenever it's convenient."

After a pause so long that Gwen had a stab of worry that she'd hung up, Lawson's mother gave her the address of a house just a few blocks over.

"I'll bring you thirty tomorrow. *Forty!* Tomorrow afternoon," Gwen said, then she added, "I'll call first." That made her sound less creepy, right?

"Amberlynn, you let go of that child! You do not want me to...!"

This time, Gwen was sure she had hung up.

Her own hand was trembling as she returned the

phone to its cradle, and she turned to find Heather gazing at her with round eyes.

"Was that…?"

"I found Henrik," Gwen said, her voice quavering like her hand had. She cleared her throat. "I found him."

"You found Henrik?" Daniella stood in the entrance of the kitchen. There was a lull in the trick-or-treaters, and her words caught the attention of the knights, who were swiftly there, demanding answers.

"Our shieldmate!"

"Where is he?"

"How did you find him?"

"What happened?"

"Is he okay?"

"How do you know?

Gwen took a deep breath to calm herself. "The kid who got hurt, Lawson, he recognized your ornaments. I got his mom's number and her address, and I'll just go and pick it up tomorrow." She managed to speak casually, like it was no big deal.

Trey and Rez gave whoops of joy, ignoring the doorbell to pound each other on the back, sweep their keys into their arms, and dance them around the kitchen. Gwen dodged back and slipped up to perch on the counter, grinning despite herself because of their contagious glee.

"Finally!" Daniella said, escaping Trey's embrace to hug Gwen. "You must be so excited."

Excitement was the smallest portion of what Gwen was feeling; she was dizzy with conflicting emotions as she hugged Daniella back.

She'd gone willingly with Robin to follow her destiny, thrilled to be part of something bigger and more wonderful than her narrow life of serving coffee and teaching little kids martial arts. The fated partner of a noble warrior, with true love like Daniella, and later Heather, had found? Yes, please!

The months since had dampened her enthusiasm as doubts crowded in: what if they never found Henrik? What if she couldn't be a proper key? What if Robin had made a mistake in finding her? The fable's power was unpredictable in this world, and they admitted that they didn't have complete control over their magic.

Now she'd find out for sure if she actually measured up, and she could feel the pending judgement like a storm on the horizon.

The doorbell rang again, and the knights abruptly remembered their candy duties, excusing themselves.

"Do you have questions?" Heather asked kindly, when the three of them were alone in the kitchen.

"I don't think I have any questions," Gwen said brightly. "I kiss the ornament and bam, naked knight. Beats hiring a stripper in a cake!"

Daniella and Heather exchanged a look that Gwen couldn't quite identify. Pity, maybe? Amusement? It was definitely at her expense.

"You'll know before that," Daniella warned her. "I saw Trey's ornament and I had to have it. Like Fabio getting a whiff of steak. I was in the middle of a job orientation, and I practically shoved Ansel out of the way to get it. He must have thought I'd had a mental break or something."

"I almost accosted a customer who wanted to buy Rez's ornament!" Heather giggled. "Like, I was fully prepared to vault across the counter and start a fistfight if they didn't give it up to me."

"So don't...you know...punch Lawson's mom in the mouth when you see her, or anything," Daniella warned her with a grin.

Gwen smiled stiffly. It was a sore point with her; when

people found out she had a black belt in karate, they liked to tease her about beating people up, but she'd never actually fought anyone off of a sparring mat. Twisted out of a few holds, maybe, but she stayed out of trouble for the most part and had never been in a place where she needed to prove her skills.

Not until she'd battled the bleak in Ansel's warehouse, and that had been an exercise in frustration as her physical sword had been able to do little damage to the shadowy creature.

"I'll try to avoid brawling with the woman who has already agreed to sell me the fragile glass ornament," she quipped.

Heather and Daniella both laughed.

"It's worth it," Heather said contentedly. "All the bleaks and dours and horrible oncoming darkness to battle, and I wouldn't trade it for the world."

There was a moment of awkward silence where they all remembered that the world might actually end with the year…and if not this year, the one after that, or the one after that.

Swiftly, Gwen said, "Well, I hope you're right, because oh my God, I will never hear the end of it from my mother if I traveled halfway across the country for a boyfriend I haven't even Internet-met and it turns out we don't actually get along."

2

*G*wen was glad for the warning that Daniella and Heather had given her the following day when Lawson's mother opened the door holding Henrik's ornament. They had offered to pick it up with her, but Gwen insisted on coming alone. She wasn't going to ask someone else to do something this important for her. Also, she didn't want witnesses if she ended up making a fool of herself.

And making a fool of herself seemed like a very likely possibility now.

The ornament in the woman's hand was wrapped in tissue paper, but Gwen didn't even need to *see* it to know that it was the glass gryphon that they'd been searching ten months for; the wave of possessiveness that swept over her was as irritating as it was undeniable. Gwen found herself feeling angry and helpless all at once, dizzy with need.

"Ornament! I'm here for the ornament!" she blurted.

Lawson's mother was understandably dismayed by her ferocious statement and stepped back in alarm, sending Gwen into a tizzy of panic. She couldn't lose Henrik now!

Not when they were this close! She was furious with herself for being so weak and so ridiculous.

Gwen stuffed her swimming emotions back down. "Sorry, I mean, we, ah, talked on the phone. Forty! I brought forty dollars! For the ornament!"

The woman paused in the act of shutting the door, eyeing the bills that Gwen was desperately waving. "It's fragile," she cautioned, not offering to hand it over.

Not supposed to punch her in the mouth, Gwen repeated to herself. "I'll be careful," she promised cheerfully.

They made the exchange like a hostage negotiation, with exaggerated, careful motions. Even through the layers of tissue paper, Gwen felt like she was taking a handful of angry bees.

Angry bees, but sexy, because she was absolutely on *fire*. It was *so* embarrassing.

"Thank you," she squeaked, and she turned and fled, certain that Lawson's mother must think she was utterly insane.

She'd chosen to walk the few blocks to pick up the ornament, and that also appeared to be a terrible mis-judgement. It had been a brief, brisk trot to get there, but going back was the longest walk that Gwen had ever taken.

She desperately wanted to unwrap the ornament and see it with her own eyes, but she feared that if holding it through layers of paper felt like *this*, if she held the bare glass, she'd arrive home soaked to the knees.

She concentrated on her goal, on the prize at the end. She'd spent the morning clearing out Henrik's room with Ansel. No one gave her any grief for insisting he got his own room, but the knowing looks could stop any time. Trey and Daniella had helped her pick out clothing for him.

She'd kiss the ornament, there would be a flash of

light, she'd explain the circumstances, they'd save the world. How hard could it be?

Really hard, apparently, because she was still half a block from the house and putting one foot in front of the other was sheer torture.

They would all be waiting in the living room, Robin and the knights and the keys. They wouldn't be unkind, but they would grin at her and look knowing, and Gwen didn't think she could face them in her current state.

So she crept around the back of the big house like a thief, climbed up on the back balcony, and snuck in through the room that Rez and Heather shared. Sure enough, the room was empty, but Gwen's secret entrance was spoiled when she ran into Robin heading the opposite direction in the hall.

Anyone else, she would have cracked a joke and squeezed past as fast as she could, but Robin's face arrested her as much as their words did.

"You...found him?"

Their voice was plaintive, uncharacteristically full of longing and grief, and they floated to a bench along the wall and sat down, hard.

No matter what was happening between her legs and spinning in her head, Gwen wasn't going to leave Robin like *that*. She sat beside them and held out the ornament. The tissue was sweaty from her hands, and it was hard to peel her fingers away.

"I found him."

Robin gave a sigh and unwrapped the layers of tissue away without removing it from her hands; it was an unwieldy size for their diminutive frame; they were about the size of an American Girl doll, and that an improvement over how tiny they'd been after the effort they had expended during the battle against the bleak.

Gwen didn't understand exactly how it worked, but something about the magic of this world was difficult for Robin to access, and as a creature entirely of magic, their stature was based on their power.

Robin called themself a fable, but Gwen's Brothers Grimm and Disney movie-influenced childhood made her think of them as a fairy, with wings that Gwen saw as translucent and fluttery, and their tiny size. A crabby, wise-cracking, gender-neutral fairy more in nature like Captain Hook than the Tinkerbell that she teased them for being, but a fairy none-the-less. Right now, they didn't seem to be interested in making jokes or trading good-natured insults.

But then, this was pretty momentous.

Gwen worried that unwrapping the ornament would crumble the last of her restraint, but seeing the ornament at last was actually better than the gnawing anticipation.

It was a deep orange-honey color, with delicate outspread wings and tiny white curved claws. A lion's tail lashed behind it, and an eagle-like head arched from the four-legged body. The white ring of glass was wrapped separately, and Robin only folded back a bit of that tissue before they bowed their head and let all of their breath out.

Were they...crying?

Gwen was unnerved and wished she could comfort Robin, but wasn't sure how. And what if she wasn't really Henrik's key and she couldn't break the spell? Certain nether parts were quite convinced, but...

"Why...why *me*?" she had to ask.

"There were two spells at work, possibly three if Henrik got off a counterspell also," Robin explained. "Multiple spells are tricky and unpredictable at the best of times...and it was surely not the best of times. Cerad and his witches cast a curse that would make the knights *fragile*, because they alone had the potential to take back the world from his darkness. I was the one who gave them a loophole for escape. Part of his spell said that no magic of our world could free them, so I found a new world, and bound them to a key that would complete them. I didn't know who my spell would find, I only knew that you would be a perfect match, a *resonant* creature from this realm, someone good at heart and brave, as they are."

They were silent a moment, stroking the cool glass, then sourly added, "And I swear by your gods that if you compare me to Merryweather from Sleeping Beauty, I will turn you into a mouse and set you loose in this house to be eaten."

Gwen had been thinking of exactly that, so she had to laugh.

"You can't do that," she challenged. "You're diminished here!"

Robin cracked their knuckles. "Do you want to find out?"

Gwen folded the tissue paper back over the gryphon. "I'm not going to take the chance," she admitted. "I've got to save the world, remember? And Socks is a mighty hunter."

Robin gave her a warm smile. "Henrik probably wouldn't be happy with me if you were half chewed up and left in his shoe," they agreed.

"That's definitely not how I imagined meeting him. I was hoping for a *few* shreds of dignity."

Downstairs, Vesta had caught sight of Socks, or perhaps a bird through the glass windows out the porch and began barking her head off. Fabio, not to be left out, added a few bass woofs while Heather scolded Vesta.

Gwen cradled the ornament into her hand. "I'd better

go do this," she said, as bravely as she could manage. "Before I lose what's left of my nerve."

Robin's small hand on hers kept her from standing for a moment. "I never meant to cause you trouble," they said solemnly. "I was trying to protect my knights and save my world's last hope, not trap you to a destiny you didn't want, and I never meant to endanger your world."

They looked up at her with fathomless dark eyes in a pale face, grim and sincere.

There was probably something kind or thoughtful or poetic that Gwen could say in reply, perhaps insist that she *wanted* a destiny, that she *wanted* to be a hero. Instead she grinned. "Sure thing, Tinkerbell," she teased them. "Let's see about this world-saving, shall we?"

Robin's face darkened into a scowl, but there was a twinkle of humor around their eyes as Gwen stood. She cradled the tissue-wrapped ornament in her hands and went down the hallway to the room that they'd set up for Henrik, just one door down from hers.

Pucker up, ornament.

3

*H*enrik was swimming through a sea of confusion. He had no body to direct, no power to control, and his helplessness ate at him. There had been a battle, he remembered. Robin had cast something. No, *he* had cast something? There had been such a chaos of spells, at least three of them colliding in a way that he knew meant trouble.

Cerad's witches, his bleak forces, the dours...Henrik struggled to remember, to focus. He was *glass*, fragile, and the light he grasped for slipped through him as if he was transparent.

He was adrift, and angry for his weakness. He was a gryphon warrior! A knight of the fallen kingdom!

He couldn't tell how long it had been, only knew that when he felt his limbs at last that they were strange and unfamiliar. He was clumsy, frustrated, and dazed, flailing wildly as life returned to him at last, feeling the unexpected brush of soft lips.

"Careful! Careful!" There was a woman before him, a

sweep of silky black hair, short around an oval face. She was back-pedaling from him, and her dark eyes were wide.

She was holding his glass prison away from them, like she was protecting it, and Henrik felt a surge of rage. Was she the one responsible for his long enchanted slumber?

"Who are you?" he growled, but when he reached for magic to persuade her to answer, he was dismayed to find that nothing responded.

A weapon then, but when he reached for his axe, he realized that he was not only defenseless, but also completely naked, and he took a staggering step forward.

"What have you done to me?" he demanded.

"I'm your key!" the woman said wildly. "My name is Gwen. Your shieldmates are here, Trey and Rez, at least, and Robin is here, too, and it's okay, we'll explain everything I brought you clothes please put them on now."

Henrik had a perverse desire to taunt her with the nudity that she was clearly appalled by, but he swiftly realized that this was only going to backfire; she must have cast some kind of seduction over her flawless skin and entrancing figure and shape-hugging breeches.

The woman—Gwen—was staring at his chest as if she'd never seen one before, and the world around them was so strange and unexpected that Henrik could not discount the possibility. They were in a fancy sleeping chamber of some kind, hung with fine fabrics and finished in metal and materials that Henrik could not identify, smooth and unmarred. Strange, smokeless lamps lit the room quite brightly, and the floor beneath his bare feet was curiously plush. A strange construct perched on a small table glared at him with what looked like blocky red numbers.

"Where am I?" he asked. Having fingers again was

unsettling, and he flexed them experimentally, rolling his shoulders and testing his range of motion.

Gwen's eyes got larger, something that Henrik had not thought possible, then screwed shut as she spun around. "Clothes!" she squeaked, pointing back at a pile of folded cloth. "There!"

Henrik could not make sense of this witch casting a seduction on him but not acting on it, but she had named his shieldmates; he would go along with her at least until he found them and got answers to his many questions.

The top garment was a simple, short-sleeved tunic in black. Holding it up, he feared it was tailored too small, but the black fabric was unexpectedly stretchy and he was able to pull it over his head and down his chest without trouble. The undergarments were similarly constructed, and more comfortable than he expected. Over this went a pair of heavy pants in a regal blue. It took him a moment to figure out the curious combination of zipper and button. There were even socks, knitted from some of the finest wool he had ever seen.

Whatever fate the witch Gwen had in mind, he would go to it well-dressed.

"I am dressed," he growled.

"Thank goodness," Gwen said, turning back. "Oh my *God.*"

She did not look much more settled, but after a moment of gaping at him, she managed a breathless laugh. "Well, that didn't help as much as I was hoping it would. Okay, then. I'm Gwen. Right, I already introduced myself. You're Henrik, welcome to Wimberlette."

"I do not know this Wimberlette," Henrik grumbled. He had considered himself proficient in geography, but he'd never heard of a place with that name, or seen people wearing clothing like this.

"You're in another world," Gwen explained, sounding sympathetic. "You came to this place, Earth, almost two years ago, in some kind of battle, and you've been imprisoned in an ornament for all that time. Robin could tell you better than I could. I'm kind of new to all the magic and enchantment stuff myself. Not as new as Heather, of course, but um...yeah."

Henrik reached again to control the lines of magic with his will and counter the spell she'd cast, because he was feeling not only base attraction to her, which might be explained by her beauty, but also a strange sense of tenderness. It must be a complicated spell indeed.

But there was simply no power, anywhere that he could sense. It was a curious and unsettling curse indeed, like being wrapped in cotton. "You said you were a...key."

Gwen drew in a shaky breath. "Yeah, a key. *Your* key. Your key to power here, I guess. I mean, Heather and Daniella are, for Rez and Trey. I'm supposed to be yours. Robin said I was. And...I mean, here you are." She laughed and gestured to him in awe. "All of you." She licked her lips. "Anyway."

"My *key*."

"Yeah. Kind of like your anchor in this world. We're supposed to...um...you know what, let's go find the others and maybe they can explain it all better than I can." She backed away into the door behind her and then turned to open it.

Henrik bowed his head to her. "I am at your command," he said, resigned.

"No," she said, turning swiftly to face him. "Not like that," she insisted, looking up fiercely. "We're supposed to be partners. Equals. I don't command, you don't follow."

"Partners," Henrik echoed.

Gwen gazed at him, looking full of longing, much as he

was, and also just as confused. "Come on," she said, and she led the way out of the incredibly smoothly-hinged door to a sunny hallway and a stairway down. He followed her hesitantly, pausing at the curious view out one of the crystal-clear windows over strange large houses in straight lines. There was light snow on the ground.

They were greeted at the bottom of the stairs by two hounds, one tall and gloriously golden, the other very small, silvery, and nervous. Both barked, clearly guarding their domain, but they retreated briefly at the call of women's voices. Then Trey and Rez were enfolding him in back-pounding embraces as the dogs swirled and barked again. For a moment, Henrik felt nothing but relief and they leaned their foreheads against each other in turn.

"My shieldmates," he said. "I see you with pleasure, though this place is very strange."

"You have only just begun to appreciate how strange," Trey told him. "Wait until you see the amazing technology they have. They have wardrobes of cold, and amazing entertainment devices. There are slots in the floor that make warm air. And perhaps oddest of all, cylinders of thin metal filled with *beer*."

"Cars," Rez interjected. "Cars are the most astonishing things."

"Cellphones," Trey suggested in reply. "Like tiny portals with whole libraries at your fingertips."

"And many mesmerizing likenesses of cats," Rez added.

The words meant nothing to Henrik. He caught himself looking around for Gwen, seeking the comfort of her closeness, and he had to stop and examine the impulse. She was, after all, a stranger to him.

He frowned. If he could sense magic, he would be able to stop the power she had over him. Power that she denied.

"This is my key," Trey introduced, drawing a young woman with pale skin and long dark brown hair forward. The larger dog was pressed up against her knees, his tail wagging eagerly. "Her name is Daniella. The hound is Fabio."

Daniella extended her hand and Henrik obediently took it and kissed her knuckles. "Oh," she said, smiling and looking amused. "It's nice to finally meet you, Henrik."

When Rez did the same with his key, a brown-skinned beauty named Heather, she forestalled his respectful kiss and explained, "We shake hands, we don't kiss them." She demonstrated.

Henrik went along with the odd gesture; it seemed impolite, but was clearly more normal in this world.

"This is Ansel," Trey introduced. "Our very generous landholder."

Ansel had the same sepia skin and deep eyes as Heather, but a shock of orange-blonde hair. "Welcome to Earth," he said with a crooked smile. A handshake was apparently common across gender, and the man's grip was firm and brief.

The small gray hound was introduced as Vesta and she danced fearlessly at Henrik's feet despite her diminutive size. It wasn't until he was kneeling to greet her that he spotted Robin. "Master...Robin? You are..."

Their mentor was not the tall, powerful leader that Henrik knew. Though they had the same long dark locks and black eyes as ever, and the same long-feathered wings, they were not even the size of a child; Henrik's gaze had gone over them several times without recognition, and he saw at once that Robin had observed him doing it.

They were standing on a low table, arms folded in a familiar way. "I am diminished in this world," they said flatly.

Henrik was already kneeling, so he remained low. "This is a strange world indeed," he said mournfully.

"Well, this is great," the key Daniella said brightly. "We're really glad we found you, Henrik. Gwen especially, I'm sure."

Gwen didn't look *especially* glad, her arms folded in a mirror of Robin's. She looked shy and uncertain, and flushed at the regard of the other people in the room. She swiftly suggested, "Does anyone else want lunch? It's been like two years since Henrik last ate, he's probably hungry."

Indeed, at the mention of food, Henrik's stomach gave a grumble to remind him of his neglect. "I would appreciate that," he said courteously.

"I will show you the kitchen!" Trey volunteered. "It is full of wonders, and the variety of foods is quite boggling."

There was another large room through a broad arch, divided into two spaces by a low counter surrounded by tall stools. In one half was a large, finely-crafted table, surrounded by chairs. In the other half…

"This is a refrigerator," Trey said, opening a tall white door to reveal a cabinet filled with chilled food.

"A microwave!" Rez showed him. "Er, do not place metal objects within it and engage it." There was clearly a story behind this warning.

"In fact, kindly do not use any of the appliances until you have been trained in them," Ansel said sensibly.

They showed him the water faucet, and instructed him in the changing of its temperature. Astonishingly, it got hot enough to scald, and cold enough to chill.

"You will delight in their drink of coffee," Trey promised, pointing out a glass carafe in a domed black structure. Everything beeped, or lit up, or blinked incomprehensible letters and numbers at Henrik.

"We're having pizza for dinner," Daniella said, edging

past Trey to close the door to the refrigerator. "How about sandwiches for lunch?"

Sandwiches proved to be a variation of what Henrik knew as a stackmeal: two pieces of bread around a selection of thin-sliced meat and cheeses, with green lettuce that was unexpectedly fresh for the cold weather apparent outside the amazing windows. There was a decadent choice of sauces to apply to it as well, and Rez and Trey convinced him to try all of them. It made for a very rich and spicy sandwich, if slightly messy.

They ate it around the large formal table, with Robin sitting at a place fashioned for just their small size atop it. Henrik was placed unsubtly next to Gwen, and he could not decide which was more distracting, the very unusual food, or the close proximity of the woman who was meant to be his destiny.

4

*G*wen stared at her sandwich and made herself eat it, hungry in completely different ways. She hated the way her eyes wanted to stray to see how Henrik was eating—even his *hands* were sexy!—and she was keenly aware of the way that everyone was pretending not to stare at the two of them. There was a knowing smile at Daniella's mouth and Heather's eyes were entirely too *blinky* to be innocent.

Rez and Trey were both grinning in joy and relief that was refreshingly uncomplicated, but they too smirked every time that she said anything or accidentally jostled Henrik's elbow.

If it weren't for their regard, Gwen wasn't sure she'd be able to eat anything. She was a tangle of emotions and desires. She wanted to show Henrik everything, tell him everything, sidle over in his lap and see what it was like to kiss him when he wasn't glass. He was so beautiful, and trying so hard to absorb everything they were showing and explaining.

He was enraptured by the potato chips that were

served with the sandwich, and Gwen could not help laughing with the others as he waxed eloquently about their crunch and saltiness.

His pickle seemed to impress him less than the chips, but he still ate it with relish that was almost embarrassing. Gwen was mortified to find that she could not even look at hers without considering body parts that had similar shapes.

"Did you get some of these *potato chips*?" he asked her politely. His shieldmates vouching for her seemed to have set his fears to rest, at least, so they didn't also have *that* awkwardness to traverse.

"I ate mine," Gwen said, feeling ridiculously shy.

He proceeded to pile more on her plate from the bowl before she could mount a protest. "They are an amazing delicacy."

"They're pretty good for generic," she said, instead of politely thanking him like she immediately thought she should have.

That led to having to explain, with the help of the knights and their keys, the idea that not only did such an amazing food exist, but that there were multiple options and grades for it.

"They have places called supermarkets," Rez said eagerly. "Bigger and grander and more orderly than any market I have ever seen, all owned by a single powerful merchant, with such wonders." He sighed.

"There are cheese-powdered chips that look like tiny clubs," Trey added. "And chips of corn in four colors."

"The cheese-powdered chips are Fabio's favorite," Daniella chuckled. "But you shouldn't give them too many treats."

Henrik nodded gravely. "This world is rich beyond

measure," he said admiringly. "I am, however, puzzled by the lack of magic."

Gwen was trying so hard not to crane her head to stare at Henrik that instead she caught the expression of guilt and grief that crossed Robin's face. She didn't think anyone else noticed.

"About that magic," she said cautiously.

Henrik turned towards her, and since they were actively talking, Gwen didn't have an excuse to look elsewhere.

He was so *golden*. His hair was long, thick curls of dark gold streaked with white gold highlights. His skin was pale gold underlaid with roses, and his eyes were brown, flecked with gold. He looked like a lion. Or a gryphon. Or a fae knight gryphon shifter straight out of a fairy tale.

"You said you were my key." Even his *voice* was golden.

"Yeah," Gwen said, only hearing after she said it how besotted it sound. She probably had the stupidest smile in the world on her face.

"I don't know what that means," he confessed.

"She is your match in this world," Robin explained, when Gwen struggled to find words. "The magic here is strange and considerably less than in ours. It has a different frequency, and you are not able to manipulate it directly. As a native of this world, she can be the bridge to your power here."

"You are a witch," Henrik said, as if a suspicion had been confirmed.

"Not really," Gwen protested.

"They don't use magic here," Rez said patiently.

"Though much of their technology is wondrous indeed," Trey added.

Henrik looked around at the table. Trey and Daniella

were conspicuously holding hands, and Heather was fussing with Rez's hair.

"Very well," he said, and he turned to Gwen and nodded. "I will accept your power."

Gwen opened her mouth and closed it again before she could answer, "I don't know how to do that."

Henrik's look turned doubtful. "But you *are* a conduit?"

"I...I guess?"

"It may take some time, shieldmate," Trey told him.

"How does it work?" Henrik asked. "Are there components to this bond?"

"It's different for each of us," Daniella tried to explain. "With us, I hear the magic and sing a harmony that allows Trey to tap the power."

Heather grinned. "I knit."

Henrik managed to look even more gorgeous when he was confused. "This is a weaving of yarn with rods, I believe?"

"I see the magic like threads of power, and I can reach up and pull them into place for Rez."

Gwen had seen it in action several times now, and it still sounded ridiculous.

Henrik turned his gaze to her as she tried to take a sip of her iced tea and she nearly wore it. She was uncomfortably aware of how close he was sitting, and how touchable his hair looked.

"How will you assist me?" he wanted to know.

Gwen shrugged and swallowed. "The only thing I'm good at is sword fighting. Robin thinks that's going to be the key to...ah...me being a key." She wasn't sure how she could possibly sound more idiotic. Daniella and Heather were both smirking at her.

Henrik looked impressed, and that had more of an

effect on Gwen than she wanted to admit. "A *sword fighter*," he said eagerly. "I did not realize you were a warrior."

"It's...ah...a technique called martial arts," she explained haltingly. "Tang Soo Do, to be specific. I've been training since I was a kid. I always liked the sword best."

"I have always preferred a battle axe," Henrik said.

"We can spar after lunch," Trey suggested. "We do not have an axe for your use, but Heather has communication with a blacksmith in the land of Georgia who will provide one."

"I am eager to cross blades with you again," Henrik said, nodding.

Gwen took another long sip of her tea, thinking entirely too hard about other kinds of blades.

5

The dishes from the meal were put into a large cabinet low to the ground that Rez explained would wash them. "Water spurts from the sides, with soap, and they emerge quite sparkling."

"Tough on grease!" Trey said, most mysteriously. "No streaks!"

"You watch too much television," his key protested.

Henrik wasn't sure what television was and he didn't want to ask. Everything here was so different and unexpected, and he felt like he was playing the fool on a stage. Everyone knew more about everything than he did, and he feared that he looked slow-headed and unworthy in front of Gwen.

He wasn't sure why he wanted to impress her so badly, but if Master Robin and his shieldmates vouched for her and vowed that she was connected to him, he had to trust it was the truth and that the confused things he was feeling would make sense eventually.

It was certainly no particular hardship to imagine the woman as his partner. She was lovely and graceful and the smile at her mouth was full of life. He wished he could kiss that mouth, see how it felt under his own, and find out if she fit as well into his arms as he guessed she would.

"Come and spar, if you are not too full and lazy now," Rez challenged, to his disappointment.

"You will find your key quite skilled," Trey warned him. "Her sword technique is excellent and her hand-to-hand fighting is beyond anything I've seen."

"I'm a black belt," Gwen said shyly.

Henrik guessed from her tone that this was a distinction of some honor, just as Gwen added, "It's...ah...a fighting rank that requires a great deal of discipline and training."

"I would be honored to spar with you," Henrik said formally.

"Come, we'll show you the garage where we practice," Trey invited, and he took Daniella's hand in his. Rez put his arm around Heather, leaving Henrick to stare at Gwen, who looked back at him with as much alarm as he was feeling. It didn't feel appropriate to take her hand or touch her, no matter how much he wanted to.

They fell awkwardly into step and followed the others out to a large attached room that was clearly set up as a sparring space, Robin flying behind.

There was a massive wheeled machine with windows showing plush couches at the far end of the space. A conveyance, clearly, but it didn't have an obvious way to hitch beasts to it, and it appeared to be pointing backwards. Beyond it was a hulking, cloth-covered shape that might have been another similar conveyance, and shelves filled with boxes.

Henrik tore his eyes away from the carriage, trying not to stare at the other strange items all around. There were curious lights and a workbench with bizarre tools, things mounted to the wall with cables and tubes that dove into the plaster walls. Above were even odder things: curved rails, and chains, and more of the smokeless lights.

There were weapons on one wall, and here at last, Henrik had a touch of familiarity. They weren't *quite* like the swords and staffs he knew, but they were close enough for comfort. There were no axes, but Trey picked him a sword that fit his hand and had reassuring heft. Gwen took up her own weapon, a small, thin sword with a long grip and very little guard.

"Heather knows some weapon-makers in the land of Georgia that were able to get us real swords," Rez explained, smiling at his key. "They are not common in this world. We have selected weapons for you and Tadra and they should be here in a week or so."

"This type of sword is more common?" Henrik asked, gesturing to Gwen's strange blade.

"Swords in general are very rare," Gwen said. "We have more range weapons. And not a lot of personal combat, honestly."

"Let us spar." The sword that Trey gravely gave him had good balance, and if it wasn't as comfortable as his preferred axe, Henrik had trained thoroughly with such a weapon.

They began with a bow, and Gwen raised her blade and waited, feet apart, knees loose. She stood like a warrior, even if she looked harmlessly soft.

Henrik gave a careful feint forward and she melted back easily and smacked back at his thrust, her blade ringing against his with more strength than he expected. The sword in her hand was held easily; she neither clutched it nor let it hang loose.

He caught himself smiling as he stepped forward

again, more swiftly, and gave two quick swings in succession.

She blocked them both, her feet quick and her arm strong, and responded with a thrust that Henrik had to step back from.

Back and forth they tested each other. She had excellent command of her weapon, but he didn't fall for her obvious traps, and she was appropriately cautious against an enemy of greater power and reach. Blade rang against blade. She always drew away first; she could never best him in a test of strength alone, but she was fast and moved in ways that Henrik didn't expect, sending flashing steel to slip past his guard.

She was a beautiful fighter, he found himself thinking. She didn't isolate her action in her arms or her feet, but was constantly in fluid motion with her entire body, moving from one thrust to a block to slip sideways out of range with a practiced dance. She used all of her weight to her advantage, always in perfect control. And she was grinning now, more relaxed than Henrik had yet seen her, which was both energizing and distracting.

He realized that he was beaming back at her, and when they ended locked against each other a moment, they *both* staggered back instead of pressing for advantage.

A scattering of applause made him remember that they had an audience, and Henrik dragged his eyes from Gwen and made a show of inspecting his blade, pulling his mouth into a frown.

"You are very skilled," he conceded, without meeting her eyes.

"Thank you," she said, every bit as formally. Then, nervously, "Did it...ah...?"

"I felt no hint of magic," he said regretfully. He'd certainly felt other things, heat rising in his veins, in his...

"A shame!" Trey said laughingly. "But perhaps if they were *alone?*"

Heather and Daniella smothered giggles.

"Perhaps if they are fighting together against a common enemy?" Robin suggested with a note of disapproval in their voice. Disapproval for the teasing? For his failure to tap into the power of this world? Henrik was unsure.

Robin was perched on a metal cylinder bristling with pipes and wires, legs folded beneath them. Henrik had still not gotten used to their diminutive size in this world. "That does seem to be how the rest of you established your bonds," they said thoughtfully.

"I would welcome a chance to cross blades with both of you," Trey said with a grin. He took down a two-handed sword and went to face Henrik across the mat.

Henrik sighed inside. He was good at fighting with a sword, but his shieldmates were considerably better and he felt worse about looking bad in front of Gwen than he did about fighting her directly. Not that he was going to admit that.

He caught the tail of a glance from Gwen as she came to stand beside him, adjusting her distance from him carefully.

Daniella, standing at the perimeter of the room, began to hum.

Henrik, suddenly hopeful, closed his eyes and cast about for the threads of power he'd always been able to draw upon and control.

It was like standing in a river in the rain, looking for a pair of dry socks.

Then Henrik heard the tell-tale rustle of Trey lifting his blade and he opened his eyes and thrust forward with his sword.

Trey easily deflected the hasty attack, but by then Gwen was already at Henrik's side, her steel flashing, and Trey had to retreat.

The fight itself was exhilarating; if fighting against Gwen had been enjoyable, it was nothing to having her at his side. She was a talented swordswoman, dextrous and swift, and they quickly established a rhythm of fight and parry. The two of them were more than a match for Trey, and Henrik smiled as they made him dance back faster each time.

Then he seemed to swell in power, and Henrik realized that the song he was hearing was not merely in his head. Daniella was singing, and Trey was moving faster, his blows stronger.

Magic.

The tide turned swiftly, and no matter how hard Henrik tried to scrabble for his own power, it would simply not obey his command. A ward, a burst of energy, a quick portal to let them jolt to an unprotected flank...nothing that he willed came to pass, and their surrender came quickly.

He and Gwen stood, defeated, and he was keenly aware of their failure.

6

*G*wen was pretty sure that nothing in the world was worse than failing so spectacularly as a key.

Henrik looked absolutely miserable, and Gwen's heart broke for him. It wasn't his fault. Maybe there was something wrong with *her*. "Well, that was embarrassing," she said loudly and jovially into the uncomfortable garage. It didn't do as much to lighten the mood as she'd hoped.

"Oh, gosh, no, you guys were great," Heather said quickly. "I've watched a lot of combat, at the Renaissance festival, and you were a great duo. I mean, really in sync."

Daniella was nodding entirely too enthusiastically. "Yeah, it was great. I mean, you looked really natural together."

"No magic, though," Robin said, and theirs were the words that meant the most. Gwen stared at them, trying to read their inscrutable expression.

"I could sense it, barely, a few times," Henrik said. "But could not command it."

"It was a worthy battle," Trey said, hanging his sword

with the others. He looked vaguely guilty, and just a little bit pleased with himself.

Gwen hung her own sword beneath his, and Henrik brought his sword to put away. There was a weird moment when they just sort of looked at each other before Gwen realized that she was standing in his way.

"Well," she said too loudly as she scooted aside. "What Earth wonders shall we show you next?" What she really wanted to show him was an inappropriate topic for the company.

"Television," Trey suggested. "I particularly like the moving art called cartoons."

"Cars," Rez countered. "We should tour the town of Wimberlette!"

"I'm not sure that he's ready for a spin out in public," Heather said reluctantly. "We should coach him a lot more before we take him anywhere."

"We do not have to exit the car," Rez said hopefully.

"You want to drive around with your head hanging out like Fabio?" Heather teased him.

"You know what you guys could really stand to show him?" Daniella said, wrinkling her nose as Trey came to give her a kiss. "A shower."

And everyone looked at Gwen again and she probably looked like a stunned fish because she was picturing Henrik in a shower and the rest of her brain was simply gone.

They had worked up a sweat during their sparring, and Gwen was abruptly aware that she was damp with perspiration, and she probably didn't smell much better than Trey or Henrik.

Not that Henrik smelled bad, exactly. Just...musky. Delicious, really. *Exciting.*

Gwen bit her lip so she had something do with her mouth that didn't involve licking him. "Okay, so one of you can do that, I need a shower of my own. Myself. *By myself.*" She looked anywhere but at Henrik as she stalked to the door into the house.

It wasn't that she didn't want to show Henrik the shower, and possibly even share it with him. But she'd just completely failed at basically the only thing a key did. If this was her destiny, why hadn't it worked? And why did Robin look so...hesitant?

She managed to forget about the dogs who'd been jailed in the house to prevent them from trying to join the sparring. She had to reach down and awkwardly catch Vesta by the collar, kneeing Fabio back as both canines tried desperately to escape from the house. Flushed and flustered, she squeezed herself through the door, shutting it behind her, and didn't glance back as she fled for the stairs.

Ansel's sprawling house had two full bathrooms downstairs, and three upstairs, one in the master suite that Ansel lived in, one in the second master bedroom that Heather and Rez lived in, and one in the middle of the house that the remaining three guest upstairs bedrooms shared. Daniella and Trey lived downstairs in the suite past the gaming room.

Gwen made it to the upstairs bathroom that she realized quite belatedly she was going to be sharing with Henrik. She undressed in her room and wrapped herself in her robe, tying it rather more tightly than she usually did, then crept across the hall. She checked to see that the door was locked twice before hopping into the shower.

She hurried through her bathing, trying not to linger over the memory of nude Henrik that was burned into her eyeballs. She turned down the water until it was almost chilly, trying to cool the irrational need that seemed to be burning into her. It wasn't just that Henrik was a Sports Illustrated-worthy chunk of muscle and curls; more than anything else, she wanted to simply fold herself into his arms, bury her fingers into his golden hair, and comfort him.

It took her much longer to tear herself out of the shower than she intended, and she cracked the door to the bathroom open feeling like a thief.

She could just hear the buzz of conversation from downstairs. The door to Rez and Heather's room was wide open and Vesta was grooming herself noisily on their bed. Gwen crept out into the hall, clutching her bathrobe around her.

"Lady Gwen?"

Henrik's door was open just far enough that Gwen could tell that Henrik had already been introduced to the miracle of indoor plumbing; he was wearing nothing but a towel and his hair was wet over his bare shoulders.

Gwen said something between a polite "Yes?" and a casual "What's up?" that managed to come out "Yulp?" Maybe he'd just think it was a thing that people of Earth regularly said, not her being incapable of simple words.

Henrik looked at her quizzically. "Pardon, but I cannot fathom how to get the undergarments from this package." He was holding a plastic-wrapped assortment of briefs.

"Undergarments," Gwen squeaked. "Yes, those are undergarments." She gave her bathrobe tie another tug, in case it was having the same thoughts that she was about yanking it off and throwing herself at Henrik. "Ah, you just have to tear open the plastic."

He turned it in his hands curiously. "You...tear it?" His other hand was busy holding onto his towel, and he couldn't seem to work out how to open it.

Gwen didn't want him to drop his towel, so she offered, "I could…"

Henrik handed her the package and watched in awe as she ripped it open.

"Is it damaged?" he asked in horror.

"The plastic? Oh, no, I mean it is, but we just throw it away. It's just...packaging."

"Packaging," Henrik agreed. He reached with the one hand to take the rolled up briefs back.

Unfortunately, Gwen had been a little too enthusiastic in opening the package, and when he took it, the plastic split and the rolls of underwear made a break for freedom, tumbling to the ground one after the other as he tried in vain to catch them. The towel was abandoned, to Gwen's chagrin, but clung to his hips anyway. She scrambled to help him catch the escaping clothing, and they nearly collided heads as they both bent to gather them up.

"Sorry!" she squeaked, squeezing the gray and blue briefs she'd managed to collect.

"I apologize!" he said, looking equally flustered.

"Here," Gwen said frantically, piling the unrolling underwear into his arms and turning to flee before the magic holding his towel at his hips failed. She pulled her bathrobe tie so tight that it cut into her waist, entirely too aware that she was wearing nothing beneath it.

"Thank you!" Henrik called after her.

Gwen tried to say "You're welcome" or "No problem," and it came out, "Your problem!"

She didn't correct herself, only scurried for her room and leaned against the shut door.

Socks was sleeping on her bed and Gwen risked being scratched to pick her up and cuddle her close.

The cat didn't struggle, only gave a sour "Mrrrwooow." When Gwen released her, she made a great show of cleaning herself in disgust.

Gwen got dressed and braved the hallway again.

Henrik had mastered his undergarments faster than she had, and she wasn't sure if she was relieved or dismayed to realize that she already recognized his laugh from downstairs. Ansel had started frozen pizzas, and the air was beginning to smell like cheese and greasy meat.

She could do this. She could face them all. She sat down on the top step, where she could hear their voices and not be seen, and tried to gather her thoughts.

Destiny had seemed so simple when Robin first found her. She wanted desperately to believe that there was some purpose for her life, and a perfect guy that she would be perfect for. Henrik was certainly absolutely nothing less than that perfect guy. He was big and surprisingly gentle and polite and smart and athletic and he moved like a lion and there was something about his slow smile that made Gwen weak in the knees.

But if this was destiny, why hadn't she been able to help him reach the magic, the way that Daniella and Heather had with their knights? They hadn't understood what was happening, so they understandably had a few rough starts, but she knew exactly how it was supposed to work...and it didn't. She remembered Robin's expression, puzzled and...doubtful. Was there some uncertainty that she was the key? The chemistry was definitely there, but what if the magic wasn't?

What if Robin had been wrong about her?

It would be just like the rest of her life, where she was supposed to be brilliant and successful and instead, she was just a barista with a bunch of second place trophies.

Gwen breathed deep and tried to calm herself. To her surprise and confusion, when she cast her thoughts to something that brought her peace, it was Henrik that she pictured first. The big, solid bulk of him seemed like the safest possible place in the world, even when everything around him made her doubt herself.

Gwen stomped down the stairs so it wouldn't seem like she was sneaking, and they all still looked up at her in surprise.

"Hey, people," she said, too jovially. "Smells good. Better than before, anyway. Now that we've showered." She was such an idiot.

"We're giving Henrik the CliffsNotes version of world history while the pizzas bake," Heather said. Vesta was in Rez's arms being lovingly scratched. Every so often he would pause and Vesta would whine and wiggle pleadingly.

Gwen told herself that was more needy than she wanted in a pet and she didn't really wish that Socks was more cuddly. She perched on the arm of the couch, ignoring the space that they'd unsubtly left for her beside Henrik.

The version of history that Henrik was getting was less 'CliffsNotes' and more 'spaghetti,' frequently stirred by questions like, "What are dinosaurs?" and "Wait, who was the poet shaker of spears?"

Gwen found herself forgetting her own self-consciousness. She'd been worried that Henrik would change the dynamic of the close friendship that had grown up around the rest of them, that she would be too wound up to be a good conversationalist. But everyone seemed relieved and happy to include him, with all the affection of family.

Then the timer went off and Ansel started taking the pizzas out of the oven.

They all talked about food over the meal, Robin perched like a king on a dais in their doll's chair and miniature table eating a slice nearly as big as they were.

Henrik acknowledged that pizza was a very fine meal

indeed, and reminisced with his shieldmates about various feasts that they had shared in the past. They regaled him with descriptions of the foods that they had found here.

"Noodles," Trey said with excitement. "A boggling variety of shapes and textures and sauces."

"Wait until you try marshmallows," Rez said eagerly. "But they really must be toasted."

"Tadra..." Henrik said after a time. "You have not been able to find her ornament?"

Everyone was silent, and Trey slung an arm comfortingly over his shoulders. "We *will*."

"I plan to dowse for her and for her key soon," Robin said soothingly. "I have recovered a great deal since I last tried."

Out of the corner of her eye, Gwen thought that Henrik looked alarmed at that statement, but he said nothing.

"I should like to assist you," Henrik said.

Gwen stuffed her last bite of pizza crust into her mouth, feeling everyone's attention prickle at her. He'd be able to assist *if* she could figure out how to be his key. Gwen set her jaw. Too much depended on this working.

"We'll practice tomorrow," she promised desperately. "Rome wasn't built in a day."

That required an explanation of what Rome was, something that Trey and Rez were both also interested in knowing. Gwen's knowledge was superficial, but Heather proved to be a good source of historical trivia, and she made a little map on the table top with geography marked in napkins and utensils around Robin's throne.

After dinner, they all cleaned up. Henrik gathered the napkins.

Gwen wrapped up the leftovers in tinfoil and was

standing up from tucking them into the fridge when he made a noise of dismay.

"I fear I have destroyed your napkins!" he said sheepishly, holding up a soaked and disintegrating napkin.

"Did you *wash* them?" Daniella asked in shock.

Gwen realized that the sound she had assumed was the knight washing his hands had been his attempt to launder the paper napkins they'd used in the sink.

Everyone in the kitchen began to chortle. It wasn't unkind laughter, but Henrik looked so dismayed holding his withered napkin that Gwen couldn't join them.

"It's okay," she said quickly, when everyone else seemed to be laughing too hard to actually explain. "Don't worry about it. It's like the plastic packaging. We only use it once and then throw it away. Here's where we put the trash, under the sink, behind this door."

Henrik looked at her gratefully and wadded the remaining napkins into a wet mass to drop into the trashcan while Trey howled and pounded him on the shoulders.

"It seems a waste," Henrik said sheepishly, ignoring his shieldmate's mirth.

"It is kind of wasteful," Gwen solemnly agreed. "For all of our technological wonders, this is not a perfect world."

They all watched television together for a while in the media room, settling on a cartoon sitcom. It required a great deal of explanation, particularly the advertisements. Gwen, who'd been maneuvered into sitting next to Henrik, was uncomfortably aware of how confused he was, and how hard he was trying. She did her best to clarify what was happening.

At the very earliest she could manage, she stood up and announced, "Well, that was fun, I'm going to turn in now. We've got a lot to do tomorrow."

All of the knights stood up respectfully as she did, a habit that Daniella and Heather had been unsuccessful at breaking in Trey and Rez.

Daniella made a show of yawning and stretching. "Oh, I think turning in early is a great idea. I'm terribly tired after all this excitement…"

"That is disappointing," Trey moped. Then he caught Daniella's eye roll and grinned broadly. "I mean, yes, so exhausted! We should retire at once!"

Rez helped Heather to her feet and kissed her hand. "I think my shieldmate has an excellent idea."

"Subtle, you guys, really subtle," Gwen grumbled under her breath. If anyone heard her, they didn't respond. "C'mon Henrik, I'll show you how blankets work."

"I am familiar with blankets," Henrik protested, but he followed her, pausing only to share a brief embrace with each of his shieldmates and gravely shake their keys' hands.

"This is your room," Gwen said, after she led him up the stairs and down the hall. "Mine is…next door." At that far end of the hall, Heather and Rez closed their door on the sound of giggles.

She took him on a brief safety tour of the room. "Those are electrical outlets. Do not stick anything in them, including yourself."

Henrik looked at his fingers as if he was trying to figure out a way to even make that work.

She showed him the light switches, now that it was dark enough to need them, and he flicked them on and off until she had to say, "That's not really good for them. Turn them off when you're done."

"Yes, lady," Henrik said humbly.

"I don't know what you sleep in. Whatever you want," Gwen said, immediately recognizing conversation territory that she didn't really want to be in. Her whole body was desperately reminding her that she was in a room with a bed. A bed and the most beautiful man she'd ever laid eyes on in her life. "A shirt, or whatever. There's extra blankets in the closet if you're cold. And you know where the bathroom is. If you need to...ah. I have a cat, and if you don't want her in here while you sleep, keep your door closed, she's kind of pushy. Her name is Socks. Very independent. You'll meet her when she's ready to meet you."

"Yes, lady," Henrik said again.

"So. If you need anything, I'm right next door." Gwen swallowed. "I'm...going to...goodnight."

"Goodnight, lady," Henrik said, and he gathered up her hand. For a moment, Gwen thought he was going to kiss it, and heat rushed through her body.

But he only shook it, formally, the way that Heather had shown him. "I am grateful for all of your help," he said in a low, sultry growl. "I feel that I have been most fortunate in the spell's selection of my key."

Words failed Gwen again. "Oh, I...that's...I'm sure I...uh...thank you?"

"Your problem," Henrik said gravely and Gwen had to flee before she either laughed hysterically or threw herself at him.

7

*H*enrik slept poorly, despite the extravagant bed with its spare blankets and multiple plush pillows.

The night seemed full of strange noises, distant rumbles and horns, and at one point, there was a nearby sputter and a burst of air that had him rolling from the bed reaching for an axe that wasn't there. He stared at the slats on the floor and remembered Trey's description of hot air distribution. Indeed, after a few moments, the air was comfortably warm. Henrik returned to the bed with a sigh of resignation.

Somewhere, a dog barked, a door slammed, and after a while, Henrik slept again briefly, waking before sunrise.

He rose and dressed in his clothing from the day before, then cautiously ventured out into the quiet house.

He paused at the door of his key. She had been clear about their sleeping arrangements. He would be in that room, she would be in this one. Was he expected to wait for her in the morning, should he rouse her, or should he go without her to the kitchen and feed himself? The door was cracked open a little, and Henrik could not decide if it was an unspoken invitation until he remembered her mention of a domestic cat.

What he really wanted to do was crawl naked into her bed and wake her with his kiss, but he knew that he didn't yet have that right.

Soon, he hoped.

He was so irresistibly drawn to the woman. Even understanding that she was his anchor here in this world, he found it unsettling how immediately he trusted her, and how much he wanted her, in ways that were both carnal and cerebral. He would have liked to ask her questions, apart from the others.

Henrik padded down the carpeted stairs and moved through the quiet common space. The castle was a marvel, with windows that let no drafts in, and smooth plaster walls in a variety of neutral colors, adorned with tasteful, under-stated art, even if some of it was bafflingly childish. The furniture was supremely symmetrical and very delicate, indicating the work of a craftsman of considerable skill.

He found the kitchen and lay his hands flat on the marbled countertop. Trey had taken great pleasure in showing him the various appliances. The cold-making food-keeper, *a refrigerator,* hulked in one corner. The draw-bridge-doored oven, currently cool, had blinking lights guarding it. Henrik skirted away from it, not willing to challenge either appliance.

The cabinets had many colorful boxes that contained things that Henrik could not identify as food. Fruity Pebbles had the encouraging word 'fruit,' but he did not think that pebbles were edible, even here. The box labeled Macaroni and Cheese did not have a smell even similar to cheese, and when he shook it, it sounded less appetizing even than the box of light rocks. Eventually, he found a loaf of bread, enclosed in a clear flexible fabric.

Remembering how Gwen had opened the package of his garments, he tore open the plastic. Thin, perfectly-uniform slices fell out once he had made an opening large enough. It was soft bread, smooth and delicious, if a little lacking in substance.

He was tucking the extra slices back into the torn packaging when there was a sudden little mrrrt! and a small form landed on the counter beside him.

It was a feline with pale fur, its nose, tail, and paws a darker brown. Its eyes were brilliant blue and they stared at Henrik in unblinking challenge.

"You are Gwen's companion animal," Henrik remembered. "Socks."

Socks made a low growl that was definitely not a friendly purr, raised herself from her crouch and paraded across the counter in front of him to investigate the bread. She seemed more interested in licking the crinkly wrapper than she was in eating the food. Her faintly striped tail lashed.

Henrik did not attempt to stroke her, remembering Gwen's warning that she was independent. "Feline mistress, please let me share my bread."

Behind them, there was a tremendous rumble and a crash that had Henrik reaching for a weapon that he still lacked. There seemed to be no source for the noise, and the cat appeared undisturbed. The kitchen was silent again, except for the cat nosing the bread packaging.

Having licked the plastic to her satisfaction, Socks threaded her way along the counter, pausing to sniff a few items and bat at the sink faucet disdainfully before she jumped back to the floor and glided away.

Henrik ate another few slices of bread and wandered

around the kitchen, not daring to touch anything. There were more of the electrical sockets that Gwen had warned him about. He turned on the light switch, unable to resist turning it off and back on again in wonder. The kitchen was transformed by the light, so beautifully illuminated that it was hard to believe it was the same space.

He left the kitchen to explore further, finding the room full of portal-like image machines where they had watched the incomprehensible entertainment. He wandered in and looked at the curious machines and black portals. The cartoons had required too much explanation for him to find them humorous. That, and he'd been too distracted by Gwen's primal nearness to pay much attention to them. All he really wanted to do was draw her into his arms, to touch her soft-looking hair, lay his lips on hers.

"Henrik?"

Gwen was standing in the doorway, and as beautiful as she'd been in his imagination, she was a hundred times more in real life. How had he gotten so lucky?

"Do you want a cup of coffee?" she asked, after a moment of silence.

Trey had mentioned coffee. "I would like that," Henrik said formally.

"I'll show you how it's made," Gwen said, and she led him back to the intimidating kitchen. She paused at the bread, open on the counter, then chuckled. "Let me get a new bag for this. Um, not all packaging gets thrown out."

"I didn't realize," Henrik said sheepishly.

"You couldn't have!" Gwen said, demonstrating the twist-tie at the end that opened the bag. "This must all be so new and weird to you." She added shyly, "It kind of is for me, too."

"Bread is new?" Henrik guessed.

Her eyes crinkled in amusement. "You," she said.

"Being your key. Do you want a piece of toast?" She was putting the last slices into the undamaged bag.

Henrik shrugged in confusion. Rez had mentioned toasting marshmallows. "Yes?"

Two slices went into slits on the top of a strange metal box and Gwen showed him the controls. "This a toaster. This dial says how dark the toast will get, we'll start about here at six. This button is for defrosting frozen things, this one is for bagels. This cancels the toast cycle. Push this lever down..." The toast vanished into the box and Henrik was astonished to peer in and see tiny wires start glowing.

"Fascinating!"

Gwen's sideways look was amused and warm, quickly changing to alarm as Henrik reached for the toaster. "Don't stick anything in there!"

Henrik froze.

"It's hot, and electrified. You could electrocute yourself."

"What is electrocute?"

"It's a painful shock, it can kill you."

Henrik eyed the toaster with new respect. "Your world is full of danger and wonders," he said respectfully. The box certainly looked harmless enough.

"Speaking of wonders, I'm going to show you how to make coffee next. This is a very, very useful Earth skill."

She showed him where the ground coffee was, and small cloth cones called filters. "You fill the pot to here," she said, pointing to a line on the carafe. "Cold water is fine, no need to use hot, and then pour it here." She let him do the pouring, and Henrik was very aware of how close to her he had to lean.

"Okay, the pot goes back here, feel that little bit of resistance? Just a little further. If you don't get it in quite far enough, you'll have a mess of hot coffee on the counter because it won't get into the pot."

"I suspect there is an analogy to be made from this," Henrik observed.

Gwen chuckled wryly. "I'm sure there is."

She showed him how to measure the grounds and insert the filter. "Did you have tea or anything?" she asked, letting him press the button that made it start to gargle alarmingly. "Something that you drank as a stimulant?"

"There were various steeped drinks that had mild magical properties. To clear the mind, to sharpen senses."

"Was everything magic? Robin doesn't like to talk about it, and the others just say that you know more about how it works than they do. Maybe if I understood it, I'd be...better at this." She flapped her hands.

"Our world is...*was*...built from magic. Magic is so deep in its roots that nothing is entirely free of it."

"Even tea?"

"A cup of tea, a table, a swath of grass, everything has a little, and there are places where it pools and flows in streams of energy. These are leylines, and I can...could...use these to act according to my will."

"So, no chanting or potions."

Henrik could not quite keep the disgust from his face and Gwen hastily added, "Okay, definitely not."

"I am not a witch, to be hobbled to spells and ritual," Henrik said haughtily. "I am a creature of magic, and I only have to will it." Then he ducked his head sheepishly. "I do find it somewhat simpler when I can focus myself physically in order to direct my intensions."

"Physically, you say," Gwen said, and she swallowed.

"Pointing at things, snapping, tracing a portal, that kind of thing," Henrik explained.

"Pointing," Gwen repeated, nodding dazedly.

He could drown in her dark eyes, if he let himself—
POP!

Henrik automatically moved to protect Gwen from the unknown source of the sudden, alarming sound, taking her arm to shelter her with his body from whatever explosion was happening behind him.

As fast as he could move, she could move faster, and he was shocked to find that his hand was peeled from her arm and rotated backwards. Her opposite hand was somehow in a vulnerable place on his elbow applying just enough pressure to assert her absolute control of the situation.

"It's just the toast," she told him, but she didn't let go, and he didn't want her to.

"You are a truly admirable combatant," Henrik said in awe.

She let go of him abruptly and color rose in her cheeks as she turned back to the counter. "Um, thanks. Here, the toast needs butter, and the coffee's almost ready."

The machine was indeed making a terrible noise, and steam and scent was rising from it.

Gwen showed him a cabinet door that revealed a collection of cups and mugs, and selected two of them. His had a photograph of a dog like Fabio that said "I'm fabulous!" Hers was white, with the image of a black belt tied around it. On the back, it read: "A black belt is a white belt who never gives up."

The bread was crisped and a factor of magnitude more delicious when it was spread with soft butter.

"We can put toppings on it, too," Gwen told him. "Jam, peanut butter, cream cheese, there's this chocolate spread called Nutella..."

"It is amazing just like this," Henrik told her. He was more enamored of the toast than he was of the coffee, which proved bitter and strong. "I fear your drink may be a taste I have not yet acquired," he told her.

Gwen suggested sugar and cream, which improved the beverage, but not enough that he took a second cup when she did.

She showed him more of the appliances in the kitchen, and when the refrigerator made another crashing noise, she didn't giggle or mock him as she opened the drawer in the bottom and showed him the *automatic ice maker*. "It makes a terrible racket," she agreed. "I have nearly peed myself more than once when it went off when I wasn't expecting it."

Henrik found himself gazing at the side of her face as she led him around the room, explaining each bizarre item and demonstrating their use. She was kind and patient, qualities that Henrik valued even above her skill at fighting and her beauty.

"My key," Henrik said, and when she turned from the blender to face him, the air between them was so charged that Henrik actually thought it was magic and was surprised when he could not touch it with his will. "My *key*," he repeated in wonder. "My shieldmates, they are...*attached* to their keys. Emotionally. Physically."

If he thought her face was rosy before, it was scarlet now, but she only said quietly, "Yes."

Henrik tried to read her expression, and decided she was, like him, equally full of both yearning and reservation. "This is very new to both of us," he said firmly. "I do not want you to feel undue pressure from the expectations of our peers."

Gwen gave a shy little laugh. "Is it that obvious?"

"They have lacked greatly in subtlety," Henrik said dryly. "But I do not wish to offer you disrespect or rush either of us. Will you permit me to court you properly?"

"Court me?" Gwen's astonishment surprised Henrik.

"I am sure you have had many suitors," Henrik said. "And my knowledge of the art is limited to literature, as I have never had the luxury of practice. I would gladly do three tasks you set me, though I doubt you will be in need of rescue."

Gwen's slow smile was like sunlight. "Three tasks, oh, that's adorable. I'll have to see if I can find a glass mountain for you to climb."

8

*I*t wasn't a glass mountain, but breakfast was definitely an uphill slide, for Gwen as much as Henrik.

Fabio came skidding out of Daniella and Trey's bedroom with a bark to raise the rest of the house. Vesta's harmony from the upstairs bedroom preceded a sudden influx of sleepy knights and keys, who gathered in the kitchen for coffee.

"Have you tried this?" Trey asked Henrik as he sipped from an alma mater mug for a university that Gwen had never heard of.

"It did not live up to expectations," Henrik replied. "I shall have water."

He got his own mug and used the filtered water dispenser in the fridge and Gwen was impressed. He was so smart and adaptable. It had to be utterly overwhelming in this strange, complicated world full of machines and technology.

Heather made scrambled eggs with gumbo flavoring and served them with an array of hot sauces that Henrik gamely tried. He turned shades of red and pronounced them 'refreshing,' but ate his final bites only with salt.

Toast on the other hand, he waxed eloquent over. "Such clever treatment! Such toppings!" He ate five pieces, slathered with a variety of choices, and declared his favorite peanut butter. The dogs begged shamelessly at his feet for the fragrant food.

Gwen sat close beside him, enduring the knowing sideways looks from the others, and he offered her a bite of everything he ate. Was this courtship? Would she know what to do with courtship if it bit her on the foot? She gamely tasted a few things, but mostly stuck to her own food, and her own thoughts.

"We'll be telling people that you're from a place called Norway," she told him, as Trey started to clear their dishes. "That was Daniella's original cover story for Trey."

"We're sunk if someone who's actually from Norway shows up in town," Heather observes. "These guys are about as Norwegian as tomatoes."

"Are tomatoes not Norwegian?" Henrik asked Gwen in an aside.

Gwen shrugged. "I don't actually know. But they were a New World food, so not originally, at least. I guess."

"New world?"

Heather, as their best historian, stepped up to explain better than Gwen could, and Gwen pulled up a map on her phone to give it some context.

Henrik stared at the phone in awe, forgetting to keep a careful space from Gwen, and she shivered as he touched it, and her hand by accident. "Oh, I have broken the portal?" he said in consternation as he mistakenly closed the map.

"No, it's okay," Gwen said quickly. "You just switched programs." She showed him the very basics in navigation, letting him hold the phone and turn it over in his big hands, fascinated.

"Rez said it had likenesses of cats."

Gwen laughed. "That's a big part of the Internet. Pictures of cats, selfies, and trolls."

"Are trolls also problematic here?" Henrik asked in all seriousness. "We battled a troublesome infestation of them once."

Gwen choked on the coffee she was sipping, realizing that he would mean literal trolls. "Er, no, these are just self-important people who are picking fights."

"I see," Henrik said, as if he didn't see at all.

"Here," Gwen said. "Let me show you the camera."

She snapped a photo of him, then showed him how it looked, to his astonishment, and for about thirty minutes, Henrik wandered around the room filling up the memory with terrible blurry photographs of mundane things. He also took photographs of his shieldmates. Trey lifted Daniella up onto his shoulder, to her laughing protest, and Heather warned Rez not to try the same.

"May I take a photograph of you?" Henrik asked, inevitably.

Gwen didn't take many selfies and she hated herself in pictures, but he asked so kindly that she couldn't deny him. "Sure," she said, shrugging as if it didn't matter.

Gwen smiled, and he snapped several shots, looking at each of the results very seriously.

"You are very beautiful," he observed.

Even if it was probably just a polite thing to say, Gwen felt her ears burn like fire. She didn't want to be the kind of person who protested that she wasn't so that he'd have to insist that she was, or the kind who accepted it as her due, so she didn't say anything.

"Oh, show him the iEarth program!" Heather suggested.

They looked at the iEarth program for a while, zooming in and out of the satellite images. Heather pointed out the place in Georgia where she was from, and Gwen showed him South Carolina.

Daniella finally pointed out the time. "We're going to head over to Ansel's shop and get Henrik some clothes and things before Gwen and I head for the cafe."

"No personal checks from you guys," Ansel teased. "Cash transactions only."

"Where's the love?" Gwen asked. "After work, I'm going to drive to Sault Sainte Marie because the game store there is getting World of Witchcraft a week before Wimberlette's store." She looked at Henrik and shyly asked, "Do you want to come with me? I can show you Canada across St. Marys." He wouldn't know what any of that meant, she realized too late.

"I would love to accompany you," Henrik said gravely.

"Great!" Gwen said cheerfully. "I'll pick you up here after I get off. Let me get my purse and hit the bathroom before we go."

As she left, she heard Henrik quietly ask, "Why would she hit the bathroom? Has it offended her?"

9

*H*enrik found the car ride deeply unnerving, but made every effort to act casual. It was normal for a metal box to roar like this. It was normal to be strapped into it with no path for escape. It was normal to be pressed up close against a woman who set his blood on fire. It was normal for the world outside to whip past so fast that it made him dizzy, and a little sick to his stomach.

When they arrived at their destination, Gwen released him from the harness, and Daniella, who had been in the front seat directing the machine, opened the door for him.

"Thank you," he said politely as he fled the terrible conveyance.

"You're welcome," Daniella said.

Perhaps Gwen's 'Your problem' was a regional response. Henrik tried very hard not to feel very small and provincial. This world was so enormous and varied.

"Coast is clear," Daniella added, and Robin flew from the car as well.

"This is where it all began," Henrik said, staring at the building.

It was not an attractive building, though it was impressively large. It had no particular grace or beauty to recommend it, but it looked sturdy and utile. This was where they had come through the veil between worlds, trapped in glass ornaments. This was where Robin had brought them, in a last-ditch effort to save their lives when they could not save their world. This was where his shieldmate had protected this world. This was where they would make their last stand.

Ansel pulled up in the allotted space beside them. Rez, who had ridden with him, seemed perfectly comfortable operating his own seatbelt and confusingly-configured door. Heather reunited with him as if they had been separated for hours instead of the mere minutes it had taken to drive here.

"I lived in this dump almost a whole year," Robin said, near his ear. "Drafty place. Not much to recommend it."

"I should have charged you rent," Ansel said, unlocking the door. "Remind me to add that to your bill. I wondered who kept stealing stuff out of my mini fridge."

"Human food isn't nearly the source of energy that fae food is, but it's strangely addictive," Robin said without apology. "And your locks weren't very hard to break."

"Remind me to add *that* to the bill, too!"

The room beyond was filled with shelving that was crowded with wonders that Henrik had never seen before.

None of the rest of them seemed impressed, but even a glance showed clothing and appliances and furniture of such varied types that Henrik was staggered. It must have taken hundreds of craftsmen hundreds of years to make so much *stuff*.

"You can hardly tell that a dragon came through the roof," Ansel said, hanging his coat near the door as he led the way in.

Henrik took off his own coat; it was cool inside, but not cold, and the ladies were looking at him expectantly.

"Let's see what we've got in your size," Daniella said. "I did a quick pass the other day to pick you out just a few things so you didn't have to wander around nude, but there was a lot more here that might suit you."

Henrik dutifully followed her to an aisle filled with clothing of all sizes and colors and materials. He picked up a pair of heavy leather breeches, but when he unfolded them, they appeared to be missing important parts; they were completely open in the areas that needed protection the most. "I do not understand these pants," he said.

"I am not buying you assless chaps," Gwen protested, taking them from him firmly and folding them back up. "Let me explain sizing to you."

"We considered purchasing that garment," Trey volunteered. "But it proved too small."

"They don't need to know that," Daniella chided.

Gwen showed him where the crafter's label was, and what the numbers meant. "Try these," she suggested, putting a folded pair of pants in his arms. They felt like a sturdy material, in heather blue, but when Henrik began to battle the button and zipper holding him in his current garb, she gave a choked noise and said, "Not *here!*"

He froze, and she grabbed several other items at seemingly random from the nearby shelves. "Here, take these, I'll show you where the dressing rooms are."

"We'll be over in housewares," Heather trilled. "Waaaaay over here."

Robin, standing on top of one of the shelves, only laughed. Ansel went to another corner of the store and began doing something with sheets of paper.

Gwen led him to a curtained alcove where he tried on each selection and modeled it for her. She seemed equal

parts embarrassed and appreciative, and Henrik found
himself posing a little more than he otherwise might,
turning at her command and rolling his shoulders. She
grew gratifyingly more flustered and they laughed together
as if they were sharing some joke that neither of them
quite understood.

Was this falling in love, this curious attraction layered
with a simple contentment being near her?

They eventually settled on more clothing than Henrik
had ever owned in his life. "What debt do I owe?" he
wanted to know. "These numbers are prices? For a form of
currency?"

Gwen took the clothing to the counter where Ansel was
working. "We use something called dollars." She took some
small paper rectangles from her purse and showed him the
lettering on it. "Will you give us a roommate discount on
these?" she asked Ansel.

"Are you an employee?" Ansel asked, bagging the
clothing. "Senior citizen? Didn't think so. Don't be cheap."

"Skinflint," Gwen muttered good-naturedly.

Henrik looked between them, and decided that neither
of them meant anything serious, though it was curious
that Ansel didn't barter. "How do you receive these
funds?" he wanted to know as Ansel took the bills and
gave back a few bills with smaller numbers that Gwen
showed him, as well as a few finely-minted coins. "Can I
participate in this purchase? I am afraid I came to your
world with nothing of value, but perhaps I can provide a
service."

"Don't worry about it for now," Gwen said, her cheeks
ruddy again. "I have a job as a barista at the same cafe
where Daniella works. That's why we look like a matched
set today, this is our work uniform."

"A...barista? That is a security detail?" It didn't look

like a practical uniform for fighting and it had no armoring at all.

Gwen gave a helpless hoot of laughter. "No, not security. I make coffee."

"This is a job?"

"It's very fancy coffee," Gwen added. "And when I go to work, I make money, and then I buy things, and people use that money to buy fancy coffee, and that's the circle of capitalism."

"It seems sensible." Henrik felt like he was missing a lot about how it worked. "You are a coffee merchant."

She opened her mouth, closed it, opened it again, and finally said, "Close enough."

"Did you find what you were looking for?" Daniella asked. "We've got to get going to the cafe. Marie's expecting us by ten."

Henrik proudly displayed the bag of clothing they had selected and they all walked towards the door, leaving Ansel grumbling over his paperwork.

"I will miss you," Trey told Daniella, bending to kiss her passionately.

They continued kissing as Henrik was keenly aware of Gwen shoving her arms violently into her coat and yanking her hat over her head.

"We gotta go," Gwen said impatiently. She glanced at Henrik, and he thought that perhaps she was expecting him to kiss her goodbye as well. He would like to, he realized, and thought that she might like it also. Certainly he was filled with the ache of knowing that she was going to go away, further than the next room. He had never been far from her in this world, and he didn't think he wanted to be.

He stepped closer, without meaning to crowd, and she

gazed up at him with a curious expression of desire and confusion and fear and dismay.

"I have to go to work now," she said. "I'll pick you up for our road trip after I'm done."

Then she turned and fled, leaving Henrik feeling quite bereft.

10

*G*wen wasn't sure how courtship was supposed to work, even in her own world. What would they possibly have in common to talk about? It wasn't like they'd seen any of the same movies, or played the same video games. Pop culture references would be completely lost on him. All of the knights seemed to get sad talking about their own world, but Gwen didn't want to spend the whole hour talking about her world and how everything worked like she was a teacher lecturing him. She liked teaching, but she didn't want that to be the sole dynamic of their relationship.

"Here," she said. "I'm going to put you in control of music." Trustingly, she put her phone in Henrik's hand. "These are the styles, each of these is a song. If you like the song, great, if you want to hear something else, we can skip it, like this. Here's a play button, those two lines will pause it."

She had to lean very close to point out how to work the controls, and was thoroughly aware of how big and *warm* he was in the cold car. The temptation to climb into his lap was almost overwhelming. Gwen buckled herself in firmly and tugged her seatbelt tighter.

Henrik held her phone gingerly as he carefully buckled himself in. "What is punk rock?" he wanted to know.

Gwen grinned at him. "Play it and see!"

To her delight, after a few minutes of Blitzkreig Bop, Henrik began to smile. "It is whimsical," he decided. They listened to Dead Milkmen and Dead Kennedys, which Henrik liked less well.

"Try the rock category," she suggested.

Henrik picked up the phone controls swiftly, and he selected the folder and started the playlist. Aerosmith's "Walk this Way" filled the car. Henrik listened raptly, skipping only a few of the songs in the mix, and asked questions about the lyrics that Gwen could only mostly answer.

It led seamlessly to talking about some of the pop culture topics that Gwen hadn't been sure how to broach, but it felt like they were having a conversation, not like it was a one-sided class. He wanted to know more about the video game they were driving to pick up, and that required explaining not only video games as a thing, but how new releases occurred and how marketing worked and even programming, which Gwen could explain only in the most general terms.

"Oh!" Henrik said in alarm. "Your phone has failed!"

They had talked long enough that it had gone to sleep, and Gwen told him how to wake it up and rattled off her passcode before she even thought about it.

Henrik happily went back to sampling music, but Gwen was thoughtfully quiet for a moment. She had never given her passcode to *anyone* before, but this felt like the most natural thing in the world.

She shot Henrik a sideways look. He was inspecting the picture of the album cover on the tiny phone screen, an adorable look of concentration on his profile. She could rationalize trusting him with her passcode by reasoning that there was very little he could do with it yet, but there was something more to her action than that. She would have given him the code even if he'd been completely competent with electronics. He was so...honorable.

Gwen guessed that she should have expected that; the knights all seemed to have a code that bound them completely.

The trip to Sault Sante Marie passed quickly, and by the time they arrived at the mall, Henrik was adept at most basic phone skills and they had listened to Queen's "We Are the Champions" enough times that he could sing along with it.

Gwen took the parking ticket and put Daniella's car into a space in the empty end of the lot. Henrik was already staring around in awe. He struggled with his seatbelt until Gwen released him, then spent a moment fastening and unfastening it so he would be able to do it himself, nodding in satisfaction when he mastered just the right amount of pressure.

"It is a mighty palace," Henrik said, looking up at the big facade of the building. "Is a mall where royalty lives?"

"No, just capitalism," Gwen said wryly. She locked the car and pulled her jacket closer around her.

It seemed safest to take Henrik by the hand so she wouldn't lose him in a crowd and he wouldn't wander off and touch things that shouldn't be touched, but Gwen wasn't entirely prepared for what that would do to her. Her whole body was aware of how close he was, how warm his fingers were, how much she loved being near him. She felt almost giddy.

Henrik seemed delighted by the contact, and he grinned down at her proudly. Then they were going in the big front doors, to a whoosh of warm air and noisy chatter, and he drew to a halt.

Gwen pulled him to the side of the stream of traffic and let him drink in the view of the busy mall for a moment. Some of the stores had Christmas displays out, despite the fact that it wasn't Thanksgiving yet, and twinkle lights sparkled everywhere. There was music playing (not Christmas music, thank heavens), layered with sounds of the air system and the escalators and the thousands of conversations and the hawkers trying to sell trendy massage pillows and squirt people with perfume.

"It is...quite an assault on the senses," Henrik murmured. Gwen wasn't sure if he was charmed or simply overwhelmed.

"The game shop is over here," she said, tugging him into motion.

He insisted on stopping and apologizing to everyone they accidentally brushed, puzzled at first by the way that they shrugged him off and hurried away. "They're just busy," Gwen explained. "They've got places to go."

"Indeed," Henrik said thoughtfully.

They stood out less than Gwen had feared. Henrik got plenty of double takes, especially from the teenage girls who were hanging out at the railings that overlooked the food court, but for the most part, people were occupied with their own business. She steered him past the hyperactive salespeople and they ducked into the game store, which was relatively quiet after the chaos of the halls.

The new game was behind the counter, and they queued up with the rest of the geeks who were excited for the release. Henrik was quiet and observant throughout the process, and Gwen gave a sigh of relief when they managed to escape the mall with no incidents greater than people being mildly confused by Henrik's courtesy.

He still seemed pensive when they got back to the car, but agreed that he was hungry when Gwen asked. "I thought we'd eat at Lock View," she suggested. "They're supposed to have pretty good food, and we can watch the ships waiting to go through. It's kind of the touristy thing you're supposed to do here."

They got seats on the second floor. Henrik held the chair for her, which the waitress clearly thought was adorable; Gwen caught her sly wink and flushed.

There were photographs throughout the restaurant of the lock being built, and descriptions of how it worked. Gwen, a careful ear out for other customers and staff, filled in some of the blanks. "Canada is another country, with different rules and government," she told him, showing him on the map.

"They are friendly?"

Gwen had to laugh. "To a fault, if anything," she said. "It's one of their stereotypes. You'd like them."

They could just see the largest of the cargo ships from their seats, waiting their turn to go through the massive locks.

"We have nothing like this," Henrik said in wonder. "The scale of your world is astonishing."

A kid from the next table stared at them, but his parents didn't seem to notice.

Gwen ordered them each the fried fish basket, and was not in the slightest bit disappointed in either the meal or in Henrik's relish of it.

"I have eaten many fish," he said. "None have been like this. How is it achieved?"

"There is a vat of oil heated to a high temperature. The fish is breaded, that's coated with a batter, and dipped into the hot oil to cook. Same with the french fries."

Henrik devoured all of his meal and half of Gwen's

french fries, and for a short time, she felt like just another visitor, on a date with a very strange Norwegian from way, way out of town. They talked about the locks, and Henrik gave the diagrams a sharp-eyed look and clicked his tongue in a weirdly bird-like way.

"What are you thinking?" Gwen asked him.

"These locks," he said, running one of his big, nimble fingers over a laminated picture on the kids menu. "It could be that this is rather how the veil between our world works. You have to wait on opposite sides for the level of the water to be correct in order to float between them."

"But Robin said that the veil was abruptly thick again, after the break of the new year."

"An imperfect analogy," Henrik agreed.

"Does it seem weird to you that the start of our calendar just happens to fall on the day that this...alignment occurs?"

Henrik's golden-eyed gaze was considering. "It seems a great coincidence."

"We've had stories of faery for a long time," Gwen said, tracing her own menu with her fingers. "They show up in almost every culture."

"Perhaps not just coincidence, then."

The waitress brought their bill with two plastic-wrapped peppermints and Gwen gave her a credit card. "You used that with the game purchase as well," Henrik said curiously.

Gwen was still explaining credit and money systems when they left the restaurant. "Want a closer look at the locks?" she invited. It was the most natural thing in the world to slip her hand into his, even though there were no crowds to battle through here and she didn't fear losing him. They walked down to the waterside, and Henrik gaped at the giant ships.

"The scale," he repeated in awe. "They are whole cities."

Gwen had never seen the locks, either, and they were both sightseers together, marveling at the scope of the engineering and wandering down the length of the shopping district, stopping to read all the informational signs and drop quarters into the telescopes.

They watched the slow rise and fall of the water until Gwen was shivering, and Henrik insisted that they return to the car.

There was a dusting of snow on Daniella's car, and they hurried to brush it off and warm it up.

On their way home, to Gwen's surprise, Henrik opened up about his own world. "We do not have wonders quite like yours," he said thoughtfully, watching the landscape zoom by. "But there are many beautiful places. The waterfalls of Aeron are considered a marvel of magic. They are as tall as one of those ships is long, and the water will heal injury and repair a despondency. There are butterflies that live only there that can leach pain from someone who is suffering, and the bird cries are a more beautiful music even than your rock music.

"The gates of Fallesh are mountains so high that no one can survive to their peaks, though it is rumored that the magic there is of such purity that no ill can be done with it."

He talked about glowing bugs like fireflies that fed on unwanted memories, and creatures like foxes with wings that could find lost things if the right questions were asked.

"Do you miss it?" Gwen asked. They hadn't bothered to put music on for their drive home; Henrik's beautiful voice was enough for her as he spoke of the world he'd left behind.

He was silent a moment, then said simply, "It has

fallen. My place now is here, to ensure that it does not happen again in your world."

When they arrived at Ansel's big house, Gwen pulled the car into Daniella's parking space and they got out and walked to the front door.

There they paused and Gwen wondered for a breathless moment if Henrik was going to kiss her before they went in.

He took her hands in his own, and looked down at her with a curious expression of longing and sadness. She tipped her head up, but he did not offer to bend down. Before she could gather her courage to *ask* him for a kiss, Fabio alerted to the fact that they were there and began baying in enthusiastic welcome. The moment was broken.

They went inside, and Henrik was immediately plied for details about the wonders of Sault Saint Marie and their outing.

11

*H*enrik swiftly realized that Gwen was not only a skilled warrior, but also a patient and capable teacher. She wore a simple uniform of white early the following day, with a black belt tied at her waist.

"When you use Tang Soo Do, it's not just about fighting," she explained to Henrik. "There are eight key concepts: courage, concentration, endurance, honesty, humility, control of your power, tension and release, and control of your speed. Some schools also add justice and connection. But it is never about hitting people or hurting them. It is about taking control of your own self and being the best person that you can, with your own body, your mind, and your spirit. We will start with a series of basic stances, and build on each form with new techniques."

She proceeded to demonstrate all of the many forms, in a seamless flow of her body, punctuated by fast kicks and punches and loud cries. Henrik could see at once control was a very key part of what she did, and it was almost a dance, as much ritual as it was a show of strength, flexibility, and speed. Henrik watched her breathe as she moved, careful and deliberate.

"Do you feel anything, as she does that?" Robin was sitting on Henrik's shoulder, observing Gwen.

"No," Henrik said regretfully. "Do you?"

Robin gave a sigh of disappointment.

They had tried several variations of her fighting technique and his, sparring against Henrik's shieldmates in different configurations, and nothing seemed to work. Everyone agreed that they fought very well together, seamlessly, even, but it was obvious that something was wrong with the *magic* end of things. Henrik was as blind to whatever power this world held as ever.

Gwen concluded her routine and bowed, then gestured Henrik to stand with her. Robin lifted off his shoulder and settled instead on the weapons rack where they could observe more safely.

"This is front stance," Gwen told him.

Henrik mirrored her and she came behind him and corrected his position, laughing. "I'm used to much smaller students," she told him.

Henrik looked back over his shoulder at her. "I do not think it would help if I crouched," he said.

They walked through the first form until Henrik could do the sequence almost as smoothly as she could, and they both looked hopefully at Robin.

Robin shrugged unhelpfully, and Henrik felt disappointed. Was this for nothing?

The door to the house opened and his shieldmates pressed through in a noisy crush, carefully keeping the dogs on the other side. Their keys were with them, and Daniella was wearing her uniform.

"I'll go jump in the shower so we can get to work," Gwen said, looking at the time on her phone.

"Any progress with your magic?" Trey asked hopefully.

Henrik shook his head. Gwen looked as defeated as he felt. "She is an excellent teacher," he said quickly. "We learned the first form and I can count to five in the language of Korea now."

She flashed him a quick, grateful smile. "You're a good student," she countered. "I'll be back down in a jiffy."

Henrik braced himself at Gwen's exit and was unsurprised to find himself the center of a great deal of amused attention.

"And how is the courtship going?" Rez wanted to know.

"It is complicated," Henrik said gravely. "I am not sure that I understand the rules very well."

"She likes you," Daniella assured him. "A *lot*."

"And I am very fond of her," Henrik agreed. He steeled himself. "But I am not sure where to go from here. Can you advise me?"

Heather turned thoughtfully to Daniella. "What do you think of a date night!"

Daniella nodded eagerly. "There's a concert in Marquette I was just thinking about trying to drag you guys to! We could make it an overnight, give them the house. Ansel's off on a business meeting until tomorrow night."

"That's not a lot of time to put it together," Heather said.

"What does a date night entail?" Henrik wanted to know.

That got him the measured look of both women.

"Do you know any poetry?" Daniella asked.

"I know the Ballad of Graycliff Battle by heart," Henrik offered.

"I do not think that will suffice," Trey said, shaking his head.

"What's the Ballad of Graycliff Battle? Do I want to know?" Daniella asked.

"It is a litany of fallen warriors," Rez said, taking down one of the practice swords. "I do not think that the lady Gwen would find it romantic."

"There's a reason that flowers and chocolates are traditional," Heather pointed out.

"I do not have funds," Henrik said dismally.

"I'll take care of those," Heather promised. "We'll get some dinner together for you..."

"Candles!" Daniella interjected. "A candlelit dinner!"

"Yes," Heather agreed. "And a chick flick afterwards. I've got just the one."

"A feat of strength may impress her," Trey suggested, coming up behind Daniella to lift her easily into his arms.

Daniella squealed and giggled happily, but Henrik shook his head. "She is a warrior in her own right. I do not think I have the skills to impress her in this way."

Rez was studying Heather, his head cocked to one side. "What does the lady Gwen like best?" he asked.

That stilled them all.

"She likes video games," Daniella suggested.

"She says she loves teaching," Heather added. "Though she may have just been trying to make us feel less terrible as students when she's dealing with our clumsy attempts. I have all the coordination of a drunk cow and she's trying to make a ninja out of me."

"You have the grace of a fall of silk," Rez protested. "It wounds me to hear you disparage yourself."

That led to a quick nuzzle between them and Robin cleared their throat and said scathingly, "Is this a dating club or a fighting practice?"

*T*he espresso machine gave a hiss of steam and a hiccup that jerked Gwen from her daze.

"Thinking about a certain gryphon knight?" Daniella asked from behind her.

Gwen groaned. "Is it that obvious?" she asked, flashing Daniella a wry smile over her shoulder and reaching for the bottle of syrup.

"It's familiar," Daniella said kindly. "I know what you're going through, remember?"

"It's terrible," Gwen complained.

"Is it?" Daniella prodded.

Gwen had to smile helplessly, thinking about holding Henrik's hand, about watching him enthusiastically discover all the wonders of their world that she'd never even thought about. "No, it's really not. Not most of it. It's just...I'm not used to dating and the weight of destiny and stuff." Her smile faded. "And..."

"And?"

Gwen sighed. "What if I'm not actually his key?"

Daniella gave her a look of sympathy. "Just because you haven't figured out how to tap into the magic yet..."

"What if we never *do*?" Gwen could hear the panic in her own voice and she stopped herself from pouring too much syrup into the drink just in time. "Robin would be the first to tell you that their own magic runs weirdly here, and I can tell that they have...doubts. What if I wasn't the key they were looking for? What if Henrik's key was that chick in the apartment next to mine and this is all just a big misunderstanding because of a ten foot error?"

Daniella's smile was warm and understanding. "You know better," she said confidently. "You have a connection!"

"How much of that is just wanting a connection so badly?" Gwen asked her, feeling a little like she was going to fly apart inside. "This isn't just about a romance, this is the pending end of the world."

"Can the end of the world wait until I get my latte?" a cross voice asked.

Gwen and Daniella turned to find a customer at the counter, looking impatient.

Gwen cleared her throat. "Ah, uh sorry," she said with a sheepish chuckle. "Just...uh...small talk." She put the cap on the to-go cup and handed it over the counter. "Sorry for the delay."

She was rewarded with a skeptical look and a slow nod before the customer left, making the bell by the door tinkle merrily.

"Well, I was able to get last-minute tickets to a concert in Marquette tonight, so I'm taking Heather and our guys on an overnight adventure. You and Henrik can have the house to yourselves and...just see where things go." Daniella looked as pleased as a cat with a bowl of cream.

Gwen looked around to make sure no one else was in

earshot this time and asked quietly, "Do you think that sex would fix things?"

Daniella giggled and flushed. "I don't know," she said frankly. "I mean, Trey and I had...ahem...well before we figured out how to tap the magic. Before we even knew what a key was. I don't think that's really the point. I mean, it's great, don't get me wrong. But the real magic is something bigger, something that's not just physical. It's this..." She fluttered her hand. "Soul connection. This deep contentment. It's the same feeling I get when I can sing just the right note. Like...triumph."

Gwen stared at her in consternation.

"Do you ever get that, when you're fighting?" Daniella asked. "Like this feeling of everything falling into exactly the right place?"

Gwen's silence was probably answer enough.

"You're really good at it," Daniella said encouragingly.

"It's a thing I can do," Gwen said helplessly. "I've trained really hard, but I've never been passionate about it like you are at singing. I've never been passionate about anything. Maybe...maybe that part of me is just broken."

To her surprise, Daniella stepped forward and enfolded her in a warm hug. "You're going to do fine," she promised. "Everything will work out exactly how it should."

"Order up!" Marie called from the kitchen.

Daniella let go of Gwen and stepped back with a kind smile. "You got this," she said cheerfully. "We still have time."

But Gwen could use a calendar, too, and she knew that the days were flipping past entirely too fast.

13

"*S*o," Gwen said, finishing the last of her food. "Do you like Italian?"

Henrik tried to decide what the word meant. "I like this," he finally offered. "It is very...creamy."

There were candles on the table, for some reason, and the far superior overhead lights were turned off. He had to squint at his strange food. Trey was correct, at least, that *noodles* were delectable. The flavored toast was a fine accompaniment.

Gwen had seemed pleased by the gifts of chocolate sweets and flowers that Heather had selected, and she laughed with Henrik when he explained why he would not be reciting poetry to her.

But if the meal was meant to be romantic, he feared it had failed.

His conversation over the meal with Gwen wasn't the easy dialogue of their road trip. Both of them seemed aware of the expectations weighing on them. They ate efficiently, talking about pets and weather and food in awkward turn. Henrik wasn't sure that a recitation of the fallen of Graycliff wouldn't have been an improvement.

After the meal, and a dessert that was rich and chocolatey and stuck on Henrik's tongue in a way that wasn't entirely comfortable, they rose and took their dishes to the kitchen. Gwen showed him how to load the dishwasher, a task that none of the others had trusted him with. The ice maker made its loud crashing noise, and Henrik barely noticed it. It was such a strange world, and its strange noises were becoming normal.

They returned to the dining room for the last dishes, and Gwen turned on the overhead light and blew out the candles.

At the end of the table was what Henrik had assumed was a thin, plastic book, but the better light revealed it to be a movie disc in its book-like cover. There was a smiling blonde couple on the front looking sidelong at each other, with a dog sitting between them. There was a castle in the background.

Gwen picked up the movie and groaned. "Look, this...isn't me. I mean, I know I'm supposed to be your perfect key, but this romantic crap, this really isn't my style. Our friends mean well, but this is just..."

"...Awkward," Henrik finished for her.

"Henrik," she said, just as he said, "Gwen..."

They stared at each other a moment.

Then he smiled at her. "You made a mighty quest for Sault Saint Marie, but you have not yet played the game you purchased there. I thought you might like to, if you are not interested in the flick of chick that Heather selected for you."

Her face softened into a surprised smile. "It's a one-player game," she said regretfully. "It would probably be really boring to watch, and completely defeat the purpose of date night." Then she added hopefully, "Do you want me to teach you how to play Zombie Killer Crew, instead?"

"This is a combat game?" Henrik said hopefully.

"Two-player," Gwen said enthusiastically. "It's really fun, and I bet you'll be good at it. No one else will play it with me anymore, but I'll go easy on you."

He followed her to the *media* room, a windowless chamber with equipment even more arcane than the kitchen. Ansel had forbidden the knights to touch anything in the room. Gwen busied herself setting up the giant screen and finding controls. Henrik tried not to gaze rapturously at her ass as she bent over to riffle through a drawer.

They sat on the couch close together and Gwen showed him what each of the parts of the controller did. The earlier discomfort dissipated before her enthusiasm.

"This is the joystick," she explained. "You don't have to tilt the controller itself, just move this little bit in the middle. See your guy move when you do that? Up there, on the screen…"

It was surreal, watching his avatar move with the commands at his hand, and the images were garish and the noise was intense. Sometimes there were explosions that sounded like they were behind him. He ran into walls a great deal, and got excited about finding tools.

"It's easy to tell the bad guys," Gwen pointed out. "The angry ones that amble are the ones you want to kill. We'll start with clubs, but we'll find something better as we level up."

"Level up?" Henrik repeated.

"It's…like a benchmark of your progress. As you get comfortable with the game, it gets harder, and your avatar gets stronger. You go up in levels."

Some of the jokes that his shieldmates had made began to make sense. *Joystick*, which was a terribly obvious double entendre. *Levels*.

It was a gripping, immersive experience, and Henrik found himself enjoying the challenge. Gwen was not impatient with his clumsiness, praising him sincerely as he figured out the basics of the system. He died with alarming frequency, but she didn't ever complain about starting over. Her assistance was both subtle and useful as she pointed out tricks and techniques.

"You don't need to lean into the controller or jerk the whole thing, even though that's something a lot of people do at first. It doesn't matter what your body is doing, just your fingers. Gaming is a finesse sport."

Many zombies fell before his blade. Many more fell to hers. They competed good-naturedly for treasure, and while Gwen did tease him, it was kind ribbing and he found himself laughing at his own ineptness.

Henrik died spectacularly once more, in a comic-gory fashion, and he collapsed back with Gwen, who let her avatar walk off a cliff and plummet into a chasm as they fell together laughing.

And then her laughter died on her mouth and Henrik was unable to resist the hunger in her eyes.

She tasted like chocolate and promise, her arms slipping up around his neck in invitation and demand. She was everything against him that he'd imagined she would be, soft strength and supple limbs. When he pulled her into his lap, she *fit* there, like he'd been made for her.

He twined fingers up under her hair and one of the controllers fell off the couch with a clatter. He was leaning her back on the wide couch, on fire with need and desire...

"Hello?"

In a flash, they were back on opposite sides of the

couch, hearts pounding and Gwen ran her fingers through her loose hair self-consciously.

Ansel appeared in the doorway. "Where is everyone?" he asked. "No one barked at me or tried to lick me, and I...uh..."

"You're back early," Gwen said too loudly.

Ansel eyed them suspiciously, noting the game end credits scrolling on the screen and their guilty demeanor. "There was an earlier flight available. I left a message on the house phone. I'm guessing everyone else is out?" He did not appear to have doubts about what had been happening. *Almost* happening.

Ansel swiftly went on, "Don't worry about me, I'm just going to grab something from the fridge and head to bed. Sorry to interrupt."

As he turned on his heels, Henrik heard him mutter, "Not like it's my own house or anything…"

"Ansel is very generous to let us stay here," Henrik said gruffly.

"Yeah," Gwen agreed, licking her lips. She looked very lost, and Henrik wasn't sure if he should gather her back into his arms. The moment seemed...gone, and Henrik was filled with regret. They put the controllers away, and Gwen turned off the machine.

They walked to the stairs and up together, their conversation trailing away as they reached Gwen's door.

Would she invite him in? Henrik desperately wanted to finish what they'd started on the couch, but he was afraid of overstepping the bounds of propriety.

"Gwen," he said softly, just as she said, "Henrik?"

He waited, patiently and politely.

"I like you, Henrik," she admitted.

"I have grown very fond of you," he confessed in return.

They were silent for a long moment and he chewed over the words. *Like. Fond.* It was a far cry from the things his shieldmates and their keys said of each other.

"We...don't have to rush into things," Gwen said quietly. "I mean, the others, they…"

"They have been decidedly unsubtle in their machinations," Henrik said wryly. "It is a great deal to handle. On top of learning about your world."

Gwen chuckled, and Henrik had to smile.

There was the easiness between them that he craved. Just the sound of her laugh made him feel like a tight band across his chest was being released. He was more than fond of her, more than simply attracted to her beauty and skill. He wanted her to be happy, to want him without the terrible pressure of destiny.

"I will retire," he said warmly as he bowed. "May your night be restful and your dreams sweet."

She looked relieved, and just a little bit disappointed, which Henrik decided was exactly what he felt. He stepped forward and laid a single swift kiss on her forehead.

"Sweet dreams," she whispered, and she fell backwards into her room and closed the door behind her.

Henrik paused only briefly, then made his way to the bathroom to take a bracing cold shower before he attempted to sleep.

14

"*I* didn't mean to be a killjoy last night," Ansel said as he came into the kitchen and grabbed a cup from the cabinet behind Gwen.

Gwen had been thinking entirely too hard about *exactly* what Ansel had unwittingly interrupted, and she tried to take a drink from her uncomfortably hot coffee to cover her discomfort, nearly wearing it in the process. "It's okay," she said, once she'd recovered her balance and kept all but a few drops of coffee in her cup or mouth. "I mean, it's not like it's your home or anything."

Ansel chuckled and poured himself a cup from the coffee pot. "Right?"

"Why are you so nice to us?" Gwen asked him as they settled across from each other at the kitchen bar. "You didn't ask for a bunch of fae knights and clueless keys to come live in your house and bust up your shop."

"You believe in fate?" Ansel countered.

"I didn't think so before this," Gwen confessed around a bite of her food. "Hard work, sure. Self-direction? But before all this, not fate."

"Do you think you're Henrik's key now?"

Gwen thought hard about the way she craved Henrik when he wasn't around...and when he was, for that matter. All the others certainly seemed convinced.

She felt like they sometimes clicked together like a unit, especially when they were playing video games, or fighting together. "I *have* to believe it," she said reluctantly.

But Henrik said he couldn't feel even a trace of magic from her, and wasn't what that a key was supposed to do?

"It's confusing," she said wryly. "What about you? Do you believe in destiny?"

Ansel gave a dry laugh. "I kind of have to. I happened to inherit a giant house full of junk and a second hand shop from a solitary great-uncle I didn't even know I had, along with an empty warehouse that just happens to be some kind of crazy pivot point between two worlds. The house just *happens* to be big enough to house a whole bunch of fae knights and their keys and their pets. The house just *happens* to have enough crap in it to keep my second-hand store stocked after it got wrecked up by a dragon and an evil smoke ghost having a battle for the future of the world."

"That's a lot of...coincidence," Gwen agreed.

"Right?"

"It's not a coincidence," Robin disagreed, appearing at the door to the open kitchen space, hovering in the air. "I suspect it was part of a spell cast from my own world."

"It was a few years before you and the ornaments even showed up in my shop," Ansel pointed out. "I don't know how it could have been a part of that."

Robin, their dark hair floating around them, settled on the counter and paced solemnly to the edge to gaze at them with their arms folded. "I do not think it was from *that* spell," they clarified. "I think it was earlier, from a spell that...I cast at another time."

Sometimes, Robin got unexpectedly cagey, and Gwen immediately recognized this as one of those times. "What kind of spell?" she asked, but she didn't think that Robin would answer.

They didn't have a chance to, as there was a sudden clatter at the door and two wound-up dogs came barreling into the house announcing their return with barks and conversational howls.

In the space of a few moments, the kitchen went from a cozy conversation to a chaos of knights, exclaiming over the wonders they'd witnessed while their keys laughingly swore that they couldn't take the knights anywhere.

"I'm not sure we'll be allowed back into any of Marriot's chain of hotels," Heather said. "And for once it's not for smuggling in a dog."

"Not that the dogs exactly helped matters," Daniella said with a chuckle.

Henrik appeared in the middle of the explanation, which involved a mistake with a microwave, a fire alarm, and also strippers that had apparently been on their way to a room down the hall.

"They were very lovely ladies," Trey protested. "But we did not desire their services."

Their story, hilarious as it was, wasn't as important as the way Henrik looked, his eyes finding Gwen before he even acknowledged his shieldmates' return.

Gwen had experienced crushes before: silly, emotional waves of desire and excitement.

But when she first saw Henrik after any absence, it was like a jolt of *rightness*. She yearned for him, wanted to fling herself into his arms with the exuberance of Fabio greeting Daniella after a day apart. Her whole body, her whole being, seemed to hum a little at the simple sight of him. The coffee in her hand was completely unnecessary.

Henrik gave her a slow smile, and Gwen was dimly aware of the others giving them suspicious and knowing looks, trying to confirm without explicitly asking what had happened—or not—the night before.

The story wound up with the keys preventing battle between the knights and hotel security, but deciding to return early anyway.

"I hope we did not interrupt anything," Rez said earnestly.

"I made you tea," Gwen said to Henrik, ignoring Daniella's wiggling eyebrows and Heather's sidelong look. "I thought you might like it better than coffee."

Henrik graciously accepted the cup with a murmur of gratitude.

The others, realizing that they weren't going to get any satisfaction, dispersed to unpack their luggage and shower.

Trey elbowed Henrik in the side as he left and Henrik looked abashed.

"I thought that I would attempt to shift this morning," he said, when even Ansel had gone.

Robin, shaking their head in tolerant amusement, agreed to Henrik's plan. "I think that's wise," they said. "If nothing else, you should be used to what you are like here."

"I'd understand if you wanted to do it alone," Gwen said, suspecting the reason behind his reluctance. The other knights had been discouraged by the way their mythical animal shapes had been diminished in this world before they had fully bonded with their keys. "In the garage, in case it goes better than you think it will?"

"I would like it if you were there," Henrik said.

"Of course," Gwen said swiftly. "No problem."

"I liked the tea," Henrik said, and his grateful smile buoyed her steps out of the kitchen.

She expected Robin to follow them out to the garage so she left the door cracked open behind them for Robin to get through more easily.

She flicked on the light switch, and the garage seemed very big and empty with just the two of them, despite the covered car at the far end. They went automatically to the edge of the sparring mats, and stood staring at each other for a long moment.

Just as Gwen was trying to find something to say to assure Henrik that he couldn't possibly disappoint her, he gave a little shrug in space and shifted.

Gwen blinked, and looked down. Far down.

And Henrik the gryphon was the most adorable thing she'd ever seen in her life.

He was smaller than Vesta or Socks, but not by much. Gwen could have just held him in her both her cupped hands, and he was an impossible amber-colored floof, with downy-soft fur over his tiny lion-like body and sleek golden feathers over his head and outstretched wings. He had an eagle's face, with a wickedly sharp-looking beak. Gwen had just enough experience with birds to suspect he could take a finger off with it.

A lion's tufted tail lashed behind him, and he stalked towards her with claws clacking on the floor before him, silent cat's paws behind. He folded his wings as he approached, his head trailing lower as he went, and Gwen could not resist reaching for him in this form, as she'd been unable to do when he was a huge and handsome human.

He did not protest when she lifted him up into her hands and cuddled him close against her neck, sighing and rubbing up against her chin.

15

*G*wen gave a sigh of contentment when Henrik curled himself against her collarbone, and he caught himself purring against her.

He'd been worried about facing his gryphon form's diminished size in this world, afraid that he would feel unwhole, that the lack of magic might make it uncomfortable. He could not help but think that Gwen would be disappointed in his small size.

But Gwen seemed delighted by his tiny form, and Henrik could feel her embrace relax as he rubbed his head against her jaw.

Henrik thought that his purr had changed in pitch, then realized that there was a new sound in the garage with them: a rumbling growl.

He cracked an eye open as Gwen swiveled her head. "What's gotten into you, Socks? Do we have mice?"

At first, Henrik assumed that the cat had taken offense at his semi-feline shape, and he stirred against Gwen's shoulder in case he needed to leap away and shift; he didn't want to accidentally hurt either of them.

But Socks had no interest in the tiny gryphon; she was staring into the far corner of the garage, past the car, growling in warning.

Before Henrik could respond, she was springing into the darkness with a predatory yowl and Gwen was climbing to her feet. Henrik clambered carefully up to her shoulder. "What are you after, now?"

There was a shrill yelp of pain, and a crash, then Socks wailed. It sounded very far away.

The furthest covered car was parked very close to the crowded corner; there was no room for a human investigation, but as a ridiculously small gryphon…

Henrik leaped from Gwen's shoulder and spread his wings, aiming for a place where he could fit between the car and the boxes beside it.

He had to fold his wings to squeeze into the space, and was instantly plunged in darkness.

At first, he thought it was normal darkness, and he blinked and paused on the hard concrete floor to let his eyes adjust.

But they didn't, and he gradually became aware of the cold that was biting into his paws. He opened his beak and gave a cry of challenge. Once, his gryphon's cry would stop armies in their tracks, but this time, it was a comparative squeak, barely a chirp. Both cold and darkness shivered back for just a heartbeat, then pressed forward again.

"Henrik!" Gwen called, and it sounded far away and muffled.

Giving up on vision, Henrik closed his eyes and stepped forward carefully, expecting at any moment to run full on into one of the boxes surrounding the covered car. He stretched out his wings, carefully, and found nothing. Behind him, the normal sounds of the garage seemed to fade away. Was it a portal? He desperately wished he could sense magic, and strained at the insides of his eyelids futilely.

A forward claw touched something soft and yielding, and there was a whimper of misery.

Socks!

Henrik opened his eyes, to no avail, and used his claws to carefully define where Socks was lying.

In his current form, Socks was larger than he was, but even if Henrik could have left Socks to suffer, he would never face Gwen again without her, so he took a grip on the back of her unresisting neck and began to drag her back in the direction that they'd come.

It was like moving through tar, or syrup; the darkness seemed to grab at them and protest their retreat, twining around his paws and tugging at his lashing tail. Socks, limp in his beak, made a low noise of agony, but didn't struggle against the indignity of being pulled along the cold ground.

Slowly, reluctantly, the darkness seemed to press less, and the cold changed from an unnatural bite to the normal chill of the concrete floor. When Henrik dared to open his eyes, they were under the car, and he could make out mysterious parts of the vehicle undercarriage, and the swirling curtain of the cover as Gwen lifted it to peer beneath.

"Socks!" she cried. "Henrik! What happened? Oh, *Socks!*"

Henrik scrambled with all four feet and wearily pulled Socks in her direction until his key could reach them both and tug them the last distance.

She cradled Henrik into the crook of her elbow and lifted Socks carefully into her arms. In the light, he could see that the cat was streaked in blackness; her paws and the side she'd been lying on looked like they'd been dipped in ink.

Henrik scrambled up Gwen's arm and leaped from her shoulder to shift before he landed.

"Is she badly hurt?" he asked anxiously.

"I don't know," Gwen said in a sob. "I don't see any blood…"

But there was clearly something amiss, because the feline was limp and unresponsive in Gwen's arms.

"I'll get Rez," Henrik said. "This is an ailment of dark witchcraft."

But Robin found him even before he could get to the kitchen.

"I found them!" the fable crowed in triumph. They had enough power again that flight was not a hardship, and they hovered at eye level, rubbing their hands together in glee.

For a confused moment, Henrik could not understand how Robin had found Socks.

They went on, "Tadra's key! I found them!"

The good news collided with Henrik's bad news in a strange mental dissonance. That would wait, right now: "Socks is hurt. Something evil has damaged her. There was a...pool of darkness in the corner of the garage. Please, we have to help her! Rez, where is Rez?"

"A pool of darkness? Here?!" Robin fluttered instantly ahead and Henrik had to almost run to keep up, hollering up the stairs for Rez as he passed them.

Robin landed next to Gwen and put a hand to Sock's head as Henrik skidded back and dropped to his knees on the sparring mat behind them. He thought that the stain marring the cat's feet had crept further up her legs while he was gone.

"Is she going to be okay?" Gwen asked helplessly, and

Henrik, without a moment of hesitation, wrapped his arms around her and held her tight.

A clatter of claws across the floor announced the arrival of Fabio and Vesta, who took the open door to the garage as an invitation and bounded at once to see their fallen companion.

"Stay back!" Gwen cried, bending to protect the prone cat and Robin, who was in the zone of their over-enthusiastic arrival. The pets swirled in confusion as Ansel and the rest of the household joined them.

Henrik felt a little like one of the four-footed companions, helpless and anxious. Gwen was hurting, and he could do nothing to help her or her fallen friend.

Daniella grabbed Fabio's collar and hauled him back. Vesta dodged out of Heather's reach and made hyper, anxious circles around them, whining piteously.

"Let me see her," Rez said, and everyone drew away from him as he shimmered and shifted.

Henrik tried not to feel jealous, remembering his own pigeon-sized form. Rez, as a unicorn, was magnificent looking, taller at the shoulder than his key, and his mane and shining horn sizzled with power. Heather stood back, making strange gestures in the air, like she was pulling on invisible strands of thread.

Robin directed Gwen to put Socks down, frowning in concern at the black marks on Gwen's hands, and she and Henrik stood and backed away. She leaned into him when he put his arms around her, and he could feel her anxiousness in every line of her body.

Rez lowered his golden horn with a touch more drama than Henrik suspected was strictly necessary, and even if he could not feel the magic around them, Henrik could see it now, glowing brilliantly around the unicorn. The stains on Socks seemed to writhe, like they were trying to crawl away to the edges of the cat's fur, as the horn drew close. Then Socks, back to her normal Siamese colors, gave a jerk of outrage and leaped to all four paws, her fur fluffed up all along her back. She shrank back from the looming figure of Rez, looked around in alarm, and streaked out of the garage before Gwen could kneel down and catch her.

Vesta, unable to resist such a temptation, raced after her and Heather dropped her imaginary strings and pelted after. "Leave the kitty alone! Vesta! No!"

Robin commanded Gwen to show her hands, which she obediently did.

"Rez?"

The power the unicorn shifter washed over the dirty-looking smudges on Gwen's hands was considerably dimmed from what he'd done with Heather's assistance, but the darkness came off as if she were washing ink off with strong soap. She rubbed them together curiously.

Robin took to the air once they were satisfied with Gwen's hands. "Where was the darkness?" they wanted to know, and Gwen pointed out the corner where Socks had vanished.

"Do you want me to move the car?" Ansel offered.

"That would be helpful," Robin said.

"Should we search for Socks?" Henrik asked Gwen, while Ansel found the keys to the covered vehicle and Rez and Trey uncovered it carefully.

"She's hiding somewhere safe and will come out for dinner, I'm sure," Gwen said, still sounding shaky as she stood. "She's very independent."

Henrik wrapped his arms around her while Ansel uncovered the car and moved it from the garage with a deafening roar, and all of them stared in consternation at what was revealed.

16

*G*wen clung to Henrik without thinking twice about it, trying to soak comfort from the solid mass of him as he murmured at her and stroked her hair.

As Ansel pulled the car forward out of the garage, the corner was exposed, and Gwen gasped and forgot about crying. "The bleak's sword…" she said in horror.

The sword they had taken from the bleak almost a year ago in the terrible battle that still haunted her memory was leaning in the corner against a stack of boxes with a hodgepodge of skis and unstrung bows and odd pieces of lumber and curtain rods and sticks of plumbing pipe. It had been a featureless black sword, matte in texture and so deep that it sucked the light away. Gwen had sparred with it a little, but didn't like the feel of it, in a purely aesthetic sense as well as a creepy suspicion that it was steeped in evil. For a while, it had hung with the other swords, but she didn't even particularly like looking at it, so she'd found the furthest corner and simply propped it out sight with the rest of Ansel's junk.

It wasn't black anymore. Or at least, it wasn't *all* black. It was as if the darkness had drained from it, inch by inch. The hilt was a colorless gray, the guard a touch more charcoal, and the blade was variegated from that to the original black-hole absence of light. Pooled around the base of it was a tarry-looking puddle, stretching under boxes and shelves and ponding out across the concrete floor. It looked like there was more of it than could possibly have oozed from a single blade.

"Ah," Robin said. They landed near the edge of the pool and knelt but did not offer to touch it.

"A great evil," Trey said gravely. "How did it come to be here?"

Gwen cleared her throat. "That would be me," she confessed, feeling about two inches tall. "I didn't like looking at it. But I really had no idea it would do *that.*"

"You couldn't know," Henrik said swiftly in her defense.

It was big of him to try to protect her, Gwen thought, and she shot him a grateful look. She'd never thought of herself as the kind of person who *wanted* protection, but Henrik's was offered without hesitation or expectation and it somehow made her feel like she mattered, not like she was worthless for needing it.

"I also did not consider such a result," Robin said without blame. They swirled a hand over the dark pool and the surface rippled like a twitch of skin that had been irritated. "Our magic works so oddly here."

Ansel returned from parking the car and went to stand next to Robin. "So...how do we clean it up? I'm guessing that Lysol doesn't make a home product for this."

Rez, still a unicorn, pranced forward with an arched neck, lifting his knees in an exaggerated parade step.

"Show off," Gwen muttered under her breath, and she was rewarded with a stifled laugh from Henrik at her side.

"A little room," Trey requested, and Gwen and Henrik shuffled over to the side with Ansel while Daniella closed her eyes and began to hum.

Gwen was not sure she would ever get used to their shifting. It was like Trey wrinkled in place, and then blurred, and then there was a dragon in the garage. He was a great, green, jewel-scaled dragon with wings that would fill the space if they weren't folded tight against his back, and he slithered forward with as much drama and preening as Rez had, his long neck curved proudly.

Gwen found that her hand was in Henrik's where they were crowded back together and it felt perfectly right. She'd rather have her little gryphon, she thought, than either of the other, showier knights.

Rez dipped his horn towards the puddle and Gwen could swear that it *growled*.

The tarry substance wriggled back from him like it was alive, the surface wrinkling. Then tendrils of black abruptly shot forward, towards Rez's feet. Daniella's song rose in volume and Trey opened a mouth full of teeth and shot brilliant white flame that harmlessly washed over his shieldmate and drove the darkness back, the surface shimmering like hot oil.

Gwen was *sure* the pool screamed then, but it wasn't exactly audible. Henrik's hand in hers tightened.

The evil tar tried to leap to the side towards Robin, who knelt unafraid at its edge. They raised a hand muttered and the darkness howled in outrage and streamed in the other direction.

Rez pranced to meet it, and he was glowing again, brightly blue, which made Gwen realize that Heather had returned. Vesta, squirming under one arm, hampered the motions of her hands.

Daniella's voice was like a bell in the acoustically poor garage, and Trey reared back for another burst of his un-burning flame.

The blackness sizzled at the edges and retreated, making several feints in all directions before it crawled, snarling, back up into the sword as Rez and Trey advanced on it.

Then it was gone, and the sword was as black as it had been when Gwen tossed it in the corner, silent and sullen. She let out a breath she hadn't known she'd been holding.

Beside her, Henrik released her hand as if he'd only just realized he was holding it and Gwen felt bereft. She dared a swift glance at him and her heart squeezed at the sight of his miserable expression.

"Is it safe to touch?" Ansel wanted to know. "How about those boxes?"

Rez ran his horn over the tainted storage containers, but Gwen thought it was only a precaution; the blackness seemed to have retreated entirely.

The knights shifted back into their human forms and returned to their keys. Heather put Vesta on the floor again and the tiny dog raced around the garage several times until she crashed into Daniella's legs and finally sat down to gnaw on her own tail anxiously.

Robin flew to the black sword and gave it a thoughtful touch. Gwen shivered to remember the feel of it in her hands. If it had done that while she was sparring with it...or when they were fighting the bleak at the turn of the year. She rubbed her hands together and wished she was still holding onto Henrik.

She felt a curious draft of air at her side and turned to find that Henrik had left through the open garage door and was walking down the long driveway towards the road.

The others were all gathered around Robin, poking at the boxes and speculating about the magic.

She chewed on her lip for a moment, then turned to follow him. She glanced once behind her, and only Ansel seemed to be watching her go. The rest were too busy to notice.

17

*H*enrik turned a random direction when he reached the road, not sure where he was going, not sure if he cared.

He wasn't surprised to hear quiet footsteps behind him, and he was less surprised when Gwen fell into step beside him. They walked in silence for a time.

There was slushy snow in some of the shaded places, but the sidewalks were otherwise bare. Houses were spaced at generous distances, with big backyards just visible through fences. Front yards seemed to be in winter mode, dead plants were pruned back in decorative beds, bushes and trees were bare. The grass that showed was brown and dry looking.

Henrik had seen *photographs* and *television* of how such places would look in summer. His head still swam with all the new terminology: *lawns* and *suburbs* and *asphalt* and *bicycles*. Everything was wonderful and fascinating...and overwhelming.

It was almost a relief to see that even here, there were seasons, and periods of rest.

"You saved my cat," Gwen said at last, when they had walked past a half dozen houses.

She was trying to make him feel better.

When Henrik could think of nothing to say in return, she went on, speaking quickly. "She won't be grateful, I'm afraid. She's kind of a snot that way. But I appreciate it. A lot. Cats are just like that, don't take it personally."

Henrik was still unhelpfully quiet, letting Gwen flounder on.

"I don't want you to feel bad," she said to her feet. "Just because they have better keys."

Henrik came to a stop. "Better keys?" he said in astonishment. She thought that the other keys were somehow *better?* Better than her indomitable will and her warrior reflexes? Better than her quick wit and her strong, lithe body? Better in any way that he could imagine?

Gwen took several steps before she realized that he wasn't beside her, then paused and turned back.

"Heather said that the bleak could choose someone, that they could link with any key that was willing. Can...could you choose someone else, do you think? If they were willing?"

The very idea of it made something freeze in Henrik's chest. "You would want me to?"

"No!" she cried. Then, more quietly. "No. But..."

Henrik stared at Gwen, realizing that his own feeling of inadequacy had been badly conveyed as something that Gwen might take as fault. *Her* fault. His fumbling courtship, his confusion with her world and her customs, she'd read these as *reluctance.*

She chewed viciously on her lower lip, and Henrik thought he knew a better use for it. "Gwen," he said firmly. "I am very..." He had to pause, searching through an inadequate vocabulary to express himself.

"Fond of me?" Gwen suggested wryly. "Look, you don't have to worry about my feelings. This is bigger than either of us. The end of the world is at stake. If I can't be your key...if I can't..."

"I am more than fond of you," Henrik said, closing the space between them.

When she would have spoken, in protest, perhaps, or to make a joke and flee, he put a finger on her ill-used lip. "*You* are my key," he said confidently. "*You* are my one. I could imagine no one more fitted to my every desire, my every dream. I could not replace you if I wanted to, and Gwen, I do not wish to. I love you. I love your wit and your eyes and your very unfriendly cat and your world, because you love it. I love your strength and your cleverness. You are my *key*," he repeated.

And it was very natural to at last bend down and put his mouth where his finger had been to kiss her.

Gwen gave a whimper and twined her arms up around his neck as she kissed him passionately back.

They might have done much more, or at least much longer, if a large, loud vehicle had not turned at the corner and pulled up across the strip of grass from the sidewalk.

Henrik reluctantly let go of Gwen and she seemed just as reluctant.

"Sorry to bother you," a man's voice called from the boxy conveyance. "I've got reports of an aggressive black dog in this neighborhood, have you seen one?" There was an official-looking logo on the side of the car-thing, and the words there read: Wimberlette Animal Control.

"No, sorry," Gwen called brightly back.

The man jotted a note down on a clipboard. "Thanks. Call it in if you see it, I guess it's been threatening local cats."

That got their undivided attention. "I'll keep mine in," Gwen promised. "And call if I see any stray dogs."

"Appreciated." The man made his machine emit a grinding noise and guided it slowly away down the road as he peered into bushes and down alleys.

There was no retrieving their previous moment in the choking wake of the vehicle's smog. Not now that Henrik could feel the worry for her cat weighing on her mind.

"I should warn the others not to let Socks out," she said, confirming his suspicion. "She's ungrateful, but she doesn't deserve to get *eaten.*"

Henrik agreed with her, and they hurried back the way they'd come.

The garage door, out of view of the house, was still wide open, despite the chill, and they went in that way and closed it behind them. Gwen looked around anxiously in the low, hidden places that Socks liked to lurk. "Hey, kitty," she called. "Socks? Let's try treats in the kitchen."

Neither of them spoke of the kiss that they'd shared, but Henrik was thinking about it, keenly. It was impossible to watch her bend down to look behind the bench in the practice area and not want her perfect, curvy little body. The feeling of her silky hair in his fingers still seemed to burn there.

The others were all in the living area and there was no way to sneak in from the garage without catching their attention. At first, Henrik thought that the buzz of excitement he sensed was just his own reaction to Gwen, but then he realized that their body language was full of relief and celebration.

Abruptly, he remembered. "Robin, you said you found Tadra's key!"

Gwen, on her way through to the kitchen, almost tripped over Fabio, who stood up exactly as she would have stepped over him. "That's amazing," she said genuinely as she shoved the hound from her path with a knee. "Where is she? Er, he?"

There was a tablet showing what appeared to be a map on the coffee table that they were clustered around. "A wondrous land called Ecuador!" Trey explained, pointing at the green and blue shapes.

"It is a lengthy distance," Robin said thoughtfully. They were standing on the coffee table frowning down at the device with their arms crossed. Their wings were folded at their back and Henrik wondered if they weren't unusually tense. "I was barely able to dowse them, and their details are...confused. I should be able to make it there without trouble, but I will need to rest a short time before I can return with them."

"You can't miss Thanksgiving!" Heather protested. "We're doing all the works!"

Robin looked gratified. "I hope to be back in time to eat myself insensible according to your peculiar customs," they chuckled. "It would be difficult for me to take a cellphone of my own, but they have robust communications in Ecuador and I should be able to find a phone that I can use if I can't manage to scry or make a portal. If I've over-estimated my abilities, we can even figure out an alternate method of transport back."

"I've got airline miles," Ansel offered, "but I don't know if they'll get you from Ecuador."

Robin gave him a grateful smile.

"Would they be able to travel as a pet?" Heather wanted to know. "They probably wouldn't need a full seat."

Trey, standing closest, gave Ansel a punch in the arm that rocked him. "Your generosity has been beyond that we could ask for."

"What are airline miles?" Rez wanted to know.

Henrik was also curious about *airline miles* (were they a local unit of measure?), but Gwen had gone into the kitchen for treats, still concerned with her feline's well-being. Henrik followed her.

"I'm excited to meet Tadra's key," she said brightly, kneeling to open the cabinet under the counter where the cat's treats were stored. "And Tadra, for that matter. Here's hoping that we can turn up her ornament faster than we found yours." She laughed dryly. "It's so funny that you were just a few blocks away, that whole time. I mean, what are the chances?"

Socks was, unsurprisingly, not in the kitchen, and did not come running when Gwen shook the little can.

Gwen wandered back out into the common area, Henrik trailing after.

"Try to keep Socks in for a little while," she cautioned the others, checking behind the couch and in all the small spaces where the cat frequently hid.

"Are you concerned for her health?" Trey asked with a frown.

"She should be in no further danger," Rez added. "But I am happy to check her for any lingering effects."

"Oh, she's probably fine," Gwen said swiftly. "But I was just out, and there was someone from animal control warning that there was an aggressive black dog on the loose."

Robin, who was frowning over a photograph, presumably of the kingdom of Ecuador, straightened in alarm. "A *black* dog?" they pressed.

"Could it be a dour?" Rez mused, clearly following the fable's train of thought.

"There are normal black dogs here," Heather pointed out. "It doesn't *have* to mean anything."

Robin frowned, unconvinced.

Gwen stood up from her fruitless search beneath the couch. "Well, either way, *try* not to let Socks out. She's got the common sense of a gerbil and would take on dours *or* dogs, as well as enspelled evil swords, and I already almost lost her once." She gave a shaky laugh. "And of course, she's lost *now*."

Henrik knew that tone of her voice, that brave timber that hid her anxiousness. "Perhaps she is under your bed?" he suggested.

"Let's check," Gwen said, and her tiny sideways smile felt like ample reward for promising to help find her pet.

18

*S*ocks was hiding under Gwen's bed, exactly as Henrik had suggested she might be, shoved into the very furthest, darkest corner with only her pale silvery-blue eyes visible. She had no interest in the treats that Gwen rattled at her, and only retreated further and growled discontentedly when Gwen tried to reach under for her.

"I could...go to your feline," Henrik suggested hesitantly. "Make sure that she remains untainted."

Gwen nodded slowly and sucked in her breath as Henrik shivered and shifted. Would he be his full, glorious size, she wondered, just as he began to shimmer. It had been a helluva kiss, and he'd said...

"I think...you're a little bigger than you were," she said hesitantly. Possibly he was, but not by much.

Henrik cocked his tiny eagle head at her skeptically and snapped his wings out in disgust before folding them down against his back.

Gwen watched him crawl under her bed. He gave a

soft little trill to Socks, who gave a little *mrrrrrt* in return as if she could not help herself.

He loves me, Gwen remembered, despite everything else that was happening. *He **loves** me.*

She should have said it back to him. She should have told him all the ways she was sure she couldn't live without him any more, about all the empty places inside that he filled. If she had, would he be too big to fit under her bed?

He seemed to be having a conversation with Socks, little tiny noises of comfort and counterpoint. There was no hissing, though the cat gave a few of her almost-spoken meows. All that Gwen could see was the occasional swish of Henrik's tail, and the blink of Socks' bright eyes. Her eyelids slowly closed, and there was a two-note chorus of purrs.

Gwen gave a sigh of relief and crawled up onto the bed. She lay looking up at the ceiling, staring at nothing and wondering why she was so wrapped up about a cat who barely tolerated her.

~

*G*wen woke up, not sure when she'd fallen asleep, to find both of them curled up beside her on the bed. Henrik had his wings tucked in tight, but one of his front claws was draped over Socks' neck where she was curled up in the curve of Gwen's side, and his beak was resting on her head.

Gwen stayed as still as she could, watching the gentle rise and fall of her cat's side and the corresponding motion in the tiny honey-colored gryphon, breathing in unison. It was so hard not to reach out and touch them, to see if Henrik's feathers were as soft as she remembered.

Socks woke with a sneeze, twitching, and sat up with a guilty look. She glared around accusingly, then stepped on Henrik's neck and angrily groomed his feathered head. Henrik opened one eye and clacked his beak but did not protest or struggle. Socks cleaned him just enough to prove some feline point, spat out a feather, stalked to the edge of the bed, and jumped down. The door was open just a crack and she walked out of the room with her tail proudly in the air.

Just as Gwen was wondering how Henrik would tolerate being scooped into her arms and shamelessly cuddled, he shifted.

He clearly misjudged how much space his human form would take, and Gwen found herself wedged up between the wall of her room and a whole different kind of wall, the bed deflecting beneath them.

"I, er, apologize," Henrik said contritely, trying to back away without actually touching her. "I should…" He rolled back off the bed and looked a little lost. "Socks seems quite recovered."

"You should close the door," Gwen said firmly.

"Very well," Henrik said, but he clearly didn't understand her reason, because when he turned back from softly latching it, he looked stunned to find that Gwen had taken off her shirt.

"I…ah…uh…" He looked like he was trying very hard not to stare at her, and failing miserably.

Gwen chewed on her lower lip and tried to smile bravely, feeling suddenly shy and uncertain. "You know, there's one thing we haven't…uh…tried yet. To get you to your full power, I mean."

Henrik sat heavily beside her on the bed, and Gwen just caught herself from falling into him. "Lady Gwen," he said, and the reluctance in his voice made Gwen's breath catch.

Did he not want her? His panting breath and his lingering looks suggested that he did. His flexing fingers implied the same impatience that Gwen was feeling, and he swallowed before going on.

"I don't want—"

Gwen's heart fell in her chest. Was she *this* bad at people?

"—to do anything you don't want to. Our friends mean well, but this must be something you truly…"

Gwen cut him off with a kiss, unable to form the words to convince him but hoping that her body would suffice. Henrik gave a growl more suitable for his gryphon form and wrapped strong arms around her as they desperately struggled closer in unison

At first, it was just hungry kissing, all but clawing at each other. Then, as Gwen thought she might burst from the pressure of her need, Henrik suddenly tipped her back onto the bed and simply held her there, gazing down with an expression of adoration.

"Yes!" Gwen cried. "Do you need me to say it out loud? In writing? Notarized? Yes, a hundred times yes, please, yes! Don't stop, don't ever, ever stop…"

Then his mouth was over hers, and his weight was deliciously pinning her and Gwen had never regretted clothing so much in her life. She got her arms up around his back and dragged her fingernails over his shirt as she pressed herself up against him. He kissed her jaw and a place under her ear that Gwen had never once even thought about but immediately decided was her new favorite skin.

She whimpered, without meaning to, and tugged at his shirt because she wanted nothing between them, not cloth, not the trappings of destiny. This was just Henrik, her glorious, golden gryphon knight, and her own raw self, offered entirely.

He took her hint at last, sitting up but still straddling her, to rip off his shirt. Then he gazed down in confusion. "I...do not know how to remove this garment," he confessed, slipping one finger under the strap of Gwen's bra. "It ties? Buttons?"

She wriggled up into a sitting position. "It clasps in the back. It's a little tricky, let me…"

Henrik sucked in his breath as she let it fall away and sat in gratifying awe for a moment before he dared to reach for her, a tantalizing finger at first, then cupping her small breast in one eager hand. He leaned forward to explore her with kisses as he pulled her closer.

Gwen was not sure what was better, the exquisite attention to her screamingly sensitive breasts, or the fact that she finally could touch the beautiful landscape of muscles that had been haunting her memory since she first kissed his glass ornament. He had shoulders like silk-covered rocks, and she didn't think she would ever tire of running her fingers over them, or of tangling her fingers in his long hair.

His mouth was as expressive on her skin as it was to his moods, and she thought that there could be no greater pleasure than the way he worshiped her with every part of him. His mane of curls trailed over skin he left burning with his wandering kisses.

"Clothes," Gwen gasped. There was too much clothing between them. She was greedy for more, insatiably hungry for all of him. "Take off your clothes!"

Obediently, he retreated from her and Gwen almost pulled him back because she wanted him too badly for logic. Instead, she began to strip herself, eager for the promise of *more*.

Henrik had clearly improved his button and zipper technique since she'd released him from glass; by the time

Gwen had wiggled out of her jeans, he was naked. Gloriously naked. Gwen dragged her gaze from his attentive cock and tipped her head up to his face.

He paused, not touching her, and it was like torture after all the exquisite caresses he'd teased her with. "Yes," Gwen said, in case he feared his permission had expired. "Yes, *please…*"

With a low groan in his throat and a snapping of teeth, he was tipping her back on the bed at last, and Gwen was spreading her legs to welcome him. "Yes…" she cried softly, not for him, but because everything in her world right now was *yes*.

She had a moment of wondering if she should be embarrassed by how wet she was, but it was brief, and driven away by the way he filled her, deeper with every thrust, until she was whimpering and biting the air to keep from screaming in release.

He drew back just at a moment that was either terrible or wonderful, Gwen couldn't tell.

"I must...I shall…"

"Yes!" Gwen commanded, clawing at his shoulders. Her orgasm crashed over her with his return, and his own desperate, pounding release spiraled her down like the notes of a familiar song.

19

*H*enrik lay in Gwen as long as anatomy allowed, holding her close against him in a blissful denouement.

She was limp with satisfaction, much as he was, with her eyes closed and her mouth curved in a helpless smile. He recognized that his own mouth must be in just such a smile; he could not quell his feelings of delight and relief.

It wasn't long before the chill in the air made Gwen shiver. The blankets were tangled beneath them, but when Henrik tried to extract one to cover her with, she sat up. "Well, that was certainly a thing. I may not relish the smug I-told-you-so looks, but damn. They told me so." She grinned at him as she swung her legs off the bed. "Want to sneak into the shower with me?"

Henrik could imagine nothing more delightful than sharing a falling water box with a soap-lathered Gwen, but he paused.

Gwen stopped in the act of standing up and settled beside him again. "You want to try shifting?" she asked hopefully. "Can you...feel magic?"

Henrik closed his eyes. "A little," he confessed, testing his perception. But none of the power he could sense would obey his whispered command. Perhaps...as a gryphon? His magic form had always been attuned to the leylines more closely than his human form.

Not sure of how much space he would need, he pushed back a table and a chair draped with clothing. Gwen crawled back up onto the bed and tucked her legs under her, watching anxiously. Henrik tried not be distracted by her beauty, forcing himself to focus. He was a magnificent gryphon, he would take up most of the empty space in the room.

When he dared to open an eye, it was as he had feared, he rattled in the emptiness and had to look up to see the top of the bed.

Gwen came to the edge and looked down at him. "You're bigger," she said encouragingly.

He was larger than Socks and Vesta, perhaps, but the hound Fabio would still stand above him at the shoulder. When he spread his wings, rather than filling the room with his glory, he could barely touch the bed and the chair at the same time.

And when he reached for the power, it slithered through his mental fingers, without substance, just as it had before. He sat, folding his wings against his back, and shifted.

"Sorry," Gwen said softly, trying to laugh. "I guess that was pointless..."

Henrik's heart twisted in his chest. He guessed that she was trying to lighten the mood, but she should not be dismayed by his failure, or try to take the fault for it.

"No," he said. He stood and padded to the bed. Gwen moved aside to let him sit, but he reached down and pulled her to her feet instead. "It was not pointless, lady, and you should not be sorry." He gazed down at her. "You are my key and I love you and I could show you with my body what words were not made for. You complete me, beloved. You are mine, and I claim you. It is not a pointless act and a knight's body is not lightly given." He took her hand into his and pressed it at his chest. "My heart is yours." He put her hand at his throat. "My voice is yours." At his mouth, it was, "My breath is yours."

Her own breath was delightfully ragged. "Henrik..."

He knelt at her feet, and then crushed her into his arms, his face just below her perfect curved breasts. "My key," he said in complete satisfaction.

They stayed that way for a time, unspeaking, Henrik taking a pleasure in her naked body against his that wasn't carnal, only content.

Then she shivered.

"The shower," Henrik said. "Let us bathe in hot water and face our shieldmates."

It was not a swift shower; Gwen was exactly as distracting as he had imagined she would be, and Henrik lingered over soaping her, and drawing the hair cream through her shoulder-length hair with his fingers.

They kissed, more than once, and though their urgency had abated, she seemed as enamored of his body as he was of hers.

"You are so beautiful," Henrik said in awe.

She peeked from beneath the towel at him. "I'm...not beautiful." She looked confusingly pleased, however.

"You are the loveliest thing I have ever laid eyes on," Henrik told her, and color rose in her tawny cheeks. "I would change nothing."

She opened her mouth and closed it again several times without speaking. Henrik was delighted by the pleasure in her eyes. He would have to praise her more often, he decided. It was clear that she was unused to admiration, and he wasn't at all sure why. She was so perfect, with her hooded brown eyes and her bee-stung lips.

"They're probably waiting for us downstairs," she finally said shyly, furiously drying the rest of her body.

Wrapped in towels, they crept back to her room and got dressed.

Indeed, his shieldmates gave him knowing looks when he and Gwen arrived downstairs, looking flushed and freshly washed. But no one said anything about it all, and the conversation centered largely around the excitement of finding Tadra's key and Robin's pending departure to bring him to their home.

20

*T*hey gave Robin a send-off the next day at the cafe where Daniella and Gwen worked, after it had closed. Robin rarely joined them on outings, because showing up with a fairy in public was even riskier than dragging around a knight who might put his fork in an electric socket at any moment.

Gwen thought Robin seemed a little sad that they couldn't be included when everyone had gone out to dinner a few days earlier, so she made the suggestion and the others had gleefully agreed. She insisted that Ansel join them, too.

As it was, the pizza delivery driver gave them a long skeptical look. Heather was wearing a medieval dress, and the knights would never look less than knightly, even in worn jeans and logo t-shirts. If the long hair and broad shoulders and courtly manners didn't give them away, there was something about their eager curiosity. Henrik was poking at a napkin dispenser like it was going to take his finger in exchange for the folded paper strip.

"I don't usually deliver to restaurants," the driver observed, as Ansel signed the receipt over their protests.

"It is a momentous eve!" Rez said merrily. "We are close to fulfilling our quest!"

That earned him a long, dubious look and the delivery driver said, "Yeah, okay," and left quickly.

"How long do you think you'll be gone?" Gwen asked Robin as the fable bent to flip open the lid of the top pizza box.

"You were pretty easy to convince," they said with a laugh. "Who knows if this one will be."

Gwen hadn't thought about the moment Robin had showed up for a long while, despite the fact that it had been a turning point in her life. Sometimes, everything that happened before she was here in Michigan trying to ready herself to be a magic knight's key seemed surreal. It felt so far in the past that it seemed like she had been someone else entirely.

She'd been such a scared girl, trying desperately to please the people around her, craving a destiny or purpose...and then she'd been handed one. Now she had friends, purpose...and most of all, Henrik.

He was peeling a string-clinging piece of sausage-laden pizza from the wheel. "How do you do this with *cheese*? You keep saying your world does not use magic."

"Do they have pizza in Ecuador?" Rez wanted to know.

"I'm pretty sure that pizza is a worldwide phenomena," Ansel said, moving the pizza aside to get the box of breadsticks on the bottom. "At least in some form."

"You want to dibs a slice of this one before these knights devour it down to the cardboard boxes?" Heather offered Ansel.

"Lactose intolerant," Ansel said with a shrug. He had

taken to writing threats of eviction on his almond milk in the fridge. "I'm on a strict breadstick and beer diet." He brandished his drink.

"Oh, duh," Heather laughed sheepishly. "I forgot!"

"How *do* you keep your girlish figure?" Daniella teased him. "If I ate carbs like you do, you'd have to wheel me to our final battle in a wagon."

"Clean living and a healthy amount of masturbation," Ansel said, with a completely straight face.

Gwen had just taken a bite of her pizza and nearly spit it out instead. The others howled with laughter and Daniella hid her face.

Henrik clasped Ansel on the shoulder. "Always good to keep the pipes clean."

"Very wise," Rez agreed.

"We are not having this conversation!" Gwen protested, when she was capable of speaking again.

"You're embarrassing our ladies!" Trey chided. "They are prudish of such subjects."

"We're not *prudish*," Daniella said defensively. "We just don't talk about these things in...mixed company."

"We *are* very mixed up," Rez observed, clearly puzzled. "Is there something wrong with self-pleasure in this world? Is it not practiced here?"

Robin was holding their sides with laughter, barely holding onto their comparatively giant slice of pizza. Daniella and Heather were leaning into each other, howling with mirth.

"You don't even have the excuse of being from a different world!" Gwen accused Ansel. "Here we were, having a perfectly normal meal—"

"No meal with this lot is normal," Ansel pointed out.

"—A perfectly *normal* meal," Gwen repeated. "And you had to go and bring up *masturbation*."

"Hey," Ansel protested. "Daniella was the one who called my figure *girlish*."

"Did she not intend it as a compliment?" Rez wanted to know.

By the time they had polished off the pizza and Ansel had taken off his shirt to hold his own in a comparison of muscles with the knights, everyone's sides ached from laughter. Robin was lying on one of the empty pizza boxes with their wings spread wide beneath them and their hands across their stomach. If there had been a pizza box in her size, Gwen would probably have joined them.

"Someone will have to carry me," Robin groaned.

"Saving your energy for the portal?" Henrik guessed. Gwen glanced at him, wondering if he sounded faintly guilty. He was supposed to be good at magic like making portals...if he had the access to the power that she was supposed to be his key to. It was her only disappointment, that no matter what they tried, they seemed to get no closer to unlocking his magic.

"Too heavy to fly."

"You know, I'm going to miss you, Tinkerbell," Gwen said frankly. "I've gotten used to having you underfoot with the pets."

Robin raised one hand with a middle finger extended.

"To Robin," Trey proposed, raising his beer. "Our mentor and master."

Henrik started to put his hand in the air with the middle finger up in imitation of Robin. Gwen caught it and shook her head at him quickly. "I'll explain that later," she promised.

They all toasted Robin, and then Ansel, for buying them dinner and putting them up in his house. "Our generous host!" Rez declared. "Selfless beyond measure."

"Oh, I'm measuring it," Ansel joked. "You'll have a

helluva bill at the end of this." He pretended to consider. "We might call it even if you save the world, though."

Gwen helped Daniella clean up the trash and take it out to the dumpsters in back as Rez and Henrik wrestled with the napkin dispensers and Trey put the chairs up on tables and swept the floor.

They paused behind the cafe, shivering in the winter air. Above them, stars glittered faintly above the rooftops.

"We'll all be together soon," Gwen said quietly. "What do you think Tadra's key will be like?"

Daniella wrapped her arms around herself; their jackets were inside and the night was too cold for short sleeves. The moon was a faint, blurry bright spot behind the clouds and there were a few floating flakes of snow in the air. "I imagine I'll like him. The rest of you turned out to be people I would have been friends with anyway."

Gwen shot her a glad smile. Whatever happened, she had never imagined the close companionship she'd found in Ansel's house with Robin, the knights, and their keys. It was thrilling to be a part of something important and to have friends that she liked and trusted.

A crash from the cafe was followed by a hasty, "I assure you I will fix it!" from Rez.

"Do we want to know?" Daniella asked with a giggle.

"No," Gwen said, laughing in reply. "But we'd better supervise the fix."

Shivering, they dashed back inside.

enrik lay very still, Gwen sleeping at one side, Socks a small immovable lump at his other.

Even though it was very quiet, Henrik thought that the great house felt as if it was crackling with anticipation.

Today, Robin would be venturing to the land of Ecuador to find the key of Tadra, and hopefully bring him back. It felt like a turning point, like a great shining hope. If they could find Tadra's key—and Tadra herself—the whole dynamic of their pending battle would change. Even if Henrik himself could not access his magic, he and Gwen were a formidable fighting team, and with Tadra's strength, surely they would be unstoppable.

He had also not given up hope that the path to his magic would become clear when they needed it most, as it had for his shieldmates.

They would be ready for this battle, regardless. He was filled with confidence and readiness.

He was also starting to feel quite trapped, between the sleeping forms of Gwen and Socks, and knew he could not work himself free without waking them.

At least...not in his human flesh.

The blanket collapsed around his diminished gryphon form and Henrik was still for a moment. Gwen stirred and tucked the blanket around her tighter, then resumed her steady breathing. Henrik swam carefully from underneath the comforter, trying not to scratch the sheets with his claws.

He was just squirming free when there was a sudden thump from above and Socks, who had apparently gone from dead asleep to predatory in the blink of one blue eye, pounced on top of him with a determined *mrrt!*

Henrik rolled, trying to free himself from both comforter and cat before he tried shifting, and Socks was on him at once, boxing with soft paws.

There followed a swift flurry of fighting, none of it very serious, as Socks tried to subdue the gryphon with claws and teeth and Henrik tried to grapple Socks into submission. Wings splayed, tails flailing, they tumbled around together until Gwen woke and rolled over.

"It is way too early for this, you guys," she said, and she proceeded to smother them with her pillow.

Socks took affront to this second assault and streaked from the bed, meowing at the closed door until Henrik shifted and went to open it for her.

When he returned to the bed, Gwen had transferred the pillow to cover her own head. "Not morning," was all she would say, curling tightly into a ball.

Henrik kissed what he could find of her head and left her in peace, pulling on the luxuriously soft sweatpants to wander downstairs and make himself toast.

He found Robin in the kitchen with all the lights still off, standing on the windowsill above the sink looking out over the morning-lit yard.

"Master Robin," the knight said respectfully.

Robin turned, the angles of their face rosy in the sunrise light. Dark hair spilled back over their half-spread wings. "Henrik," they said with a formal nod.

"Robin," Henrik said again, hesitantly.

Robin floated to the counter and walked to touch their forehead to Henrik's.

Bending so close, Henrik thought that Robin looked weary and troubled. "I am sorry, Master."

"Sorry?" Robin asked swiftly.

"I am not capable of magic here. If I could, I would take some of this burden from you..."

Robin's small hands on Henrik's cheeks were stronger than their size suggested. It was strange, compared to Henrik's memories of being young, comforted by the larger-than-life Robin and wrapped in their feathered wings. "It is not your burden. Do not feel bad for these circumstances."

"But if I were..."

Robin still had sufficient strength to tweak his nose as if Henrik were only a child.

"I did not teach you to wallow in regrets and would-bes," they said firmly. "Now, are you going to make us some grub or whine like a spoiled princess about how unfair life is?"

Henrik had to laugh, as he went to collect the bread from the cabinet. "Let me make us some breakfast."

He gave Robin a corner of his toast and jam, and the others found them at the kitchen bar laughing over Robin's droll retelling of a story called "It's Thanksgiving, Charlie Brown."

"We're not going to make this a big send-off," Robin told them. "We got all that sappy crap out of the way last night."

Trey leaned over to press his forehead with Robin's and received a pinch for his trouble.

"Troublesome *fairy*," Trey responded fondly.

"Is it time for Tinkerbell's farewell speech?" Gwen came up behind Henrik and wrapped her arms around him for a quick hug. She didn't look much more awake than she had when he had left her in their bed. Henrik dropped a kiss on the crown of her head.

"I'll need a tablet," Robin said. "For a photograph."

Daniella provided the device and called up the location program, placing it flat on the table next to Robin.

Henrik frowned to think that at one point, he could have effortlessly scried the information that Robin relied on technology for, and Gwen slipped her hand into his and squeezed it. She felt as he did, the weight of the expectations on them, and the guilt of being incapable of unlocking his magic. He smiled down at her, bittersweet. They shared even *this*.

"I've got the place," Robin said, standing taller after a moment of study. They murmured a few words, as Henrik strained in vain to *feel* what was happening.

Their magic became visible after just a few moments, and a small rip in space cracked and spread open just where Robin willed it, accompanied by a snap of sound. Green jungle was visible through the portal, swaying in a warm breeze that seemed to brighten the room. They paused a moment, and Henrik was dismayed by how winded the fable looked for such a small portal. How much would this effort diminish them? How much should Henrik have been able to spare them?

"Goodbye, Robin!" he said swiftly, and the others chorused quick farewells, not wanting to delay the fable.

"See you before Thanksgiving," Robin promised. "Don't have too much fun without me."

"Take care, Tinkerbell!" Gwen called, just as they stepped through the shimmering space.

Robin took the time to lift a middle finger at her before they pulled the portal closed behind them.

The end of the world seemed very far away indeed, and Gwen felt as though she ought to be afraid, or feel bad, or at the very least be drowning in the guilt that she couldn't be a proper key. No matter how they tried sparring, she couldn't feed magic to Henrik, and it ought to keep her up at night with shame and worry.

But instead, it felt like the tiniest fly in the biggest jar of ointment in the world and Gwen was deliriously happy. Henrik loved her. Whatever happened, however she worked out as a key, Henrik adored her and she adored him right back, every bit as hard. It definitely wasn't shame and worry that were keeping her up at night as much as it was sharing her bed with someone she didn't want to sleep through.

She couldn't get enough of him, and it wasn't just the sex. Though no one else had ever set her on fire like he could, it was even better sharing all her favorite things with him. He didn't find her interests boring or pointless, and he picked up everything she taught him impressively quickly. Gwen was sure that she'd have been twice as helpless in his world, but within a few weeks, Henrik was gliding through everyday life as if he'd always had running water and electricity. He only set one minor fire, trying to make toast on her hair dryer, and he'd quickly doused it; Ansel had put up three extra fire extinguishers the first week that Rez moved in with Heather and made a point of showing the knights how to use them.

They went for long walks through the neighborhood, sometimes bringing Fabio with them. She took the knight out to see a movie in the theater and spent the entire time staring at his enraptured face, feeding him popcorn and explaining the incomprehensible parts. They stopped even pretending to have separate bedrooms after the first night; Henrik had no possessions to speak of, and he fit as perfectly in her room as the rest of him fit in her heart.

"I can't believe my cat likes you more than me," Gwen groused good-naturedly. They were sitting together on the couch in the media room and Socks was sitting on Henrik's lap, purring and kneading her claws through his jeans into his thighs. He was stoically pretending it didn't hurt, but every so often he'd wince. "You don't have to let her do that, you know."

"It is an expression of her affection," Henrik said nobly. "I accept the discomfort as the price of her trust."

Gwen reached over to stroke Socks' smoke-colored ears and was rewarded with an unamused gaze and a momentary stutter to her purr. She resumed her game and Socks continued her steady rumble of grudging pleasure.

"You are very good at this," Henrik observed after a few moments. "This game is very different than the one we play."

"It's about seeing patterns," Gwen explained. "Once you understand the mechanics, you just keep your eyes out for the anomalies and follow the clues."

She pointed out what she was doing as they went along, which was an interesting exercise in recognizing a lot of what she did instinctively. "See, there's a gap in the wall there, that's going to mean something. Yup, there's another hellbeast. Let's get rid of that." She jiggled the tiny joystick with a thumb and activated her weapons with the buttons.

"Clever!" Henrik said, and she didn't think that he was saying it ironically.

"I thought about going into game design out of high school," Gwen admitted. "I really like solving logic problems and it's nice having a world that you can control, you know?"

"That I do understand," Henrik said gravely, and she spared a glance from the screen to see him looking sadly down at one hand. He shook his head. "But you did not do this...thing of school?"

"Game design isn't all that respectable," Gwen said wryly. "Everyone in my family thought it was a terrible idea."

"You chose to honor the choices of others for your life."

"That's a nice way of saying I'm a pushover. I got a perfectly honorable degree in math and later took a job as a barista because it turns out I actually hated math."

It came out more bitter than Gwen intended, and she viciously mowed down several hellbeasts with her bladed weed wacker. "You probably ended up being exactly what your parents wanted of you," she added. "Mr. Perfect-hair, Defender of the Crown, Tight-pants Fae Knight."

"I did not have parents," Henrik said mournfully.

Oh, way to go, Gwen, she told herself. *Bring up his dead parents, why don't you.* It was a topic that hadn't come up before and now she thought she understood why.

"I'm sorry," she said gently. "Did they...ah...die when you were young?"

"I never knew them," Henrik said. "We were raised by Robin, and trained from a very young age for our destiny."

"That's a lot of pressure," Gwen observed.

"We were worthy," Henrik said, but Gwen thought he sounded a little uncertain.

She paused the game. "Tell me about magic. How does it work? Maybe if I knew more about it, I could see or hear it like the others can."

Henrik shifted so that they were facing each other. Socks didn't flee, but she did protest the jostling. "I can only tell you with any certainty how it works in my own world." He gestured at the screen. "I don't know if you have the same...er...operating system?"

"That's a perfect analogy," Gwen said admiringly. Sometimes she was awed by how quickly he picked things up.

"Our world is a place made of light and magic," Henrik said. "Or at least, it was. Humans lived in the shelter of this magic and there was harmony. But some of the humans coveted the magic for themselves, and they learned to manipulate it with spells and tools and to use it for themselves."

"Witches," Gwen guessed. She'd heard the other knights use the term, and not terribly flatteringly.

"Witches," Henrik agreed. "But when they used the leylines, they drained them, and I don't know about your world, but ours cannot live without its magic. When *we* use magic, we do not use it up, we only bend it to our will, like mirrors with light. Dark sorcerers burn it, like flame from a candle draws wax, and leave behind faint shades of chaos, which you have met as dours. At first it was a slow drain, barely perceptible in the great well of our world, and dours were few. But there was a man, an evil man, Cerad, who wanted to harness its full strength. He figured out how to control the dours, and how to turn human hosts to his will."

"Bleaks." Gwen had fought bleaks. "They are human?"

"*Were* human," Henrik said firmly. "They are the burnt-out shells of the humans that were, nothing now but ash and ill, shaped to the command of Cerad."

"That's not creepy at all," Gwen muttered. "So when you're in your own world, how do you use magic?"

Henrik looked out into space, rather wistfully. "In my own world, everything around me is flowing with magic, and I have only to reach out and whisper it a command to make it do as I wish."

"Okay, like...portals and dowsing. I've seen those. What about...like I don't know, love potions? Or truth spells?"

"We did not have a need for such things," Henrik said mournfully. "All *was* love and truth before the Crown was broken."

"The crown was what...your king?"

"Our leader, yes. A benevolent force of justice and peace, the source and protection of all of our world's magic. With the fall of the crown, Cerad gained access to all of it, and poisoned it at the source. Robin says that by the time we escaped that even the deep magic had been tainted, that we had...already failed."

"Deep magic?"

"Like source water for the leylines. Power so pure and strong that it held the pillars of our world aloft."

Gwen eyed him curiously. Was it metaphorical, or did he actually come from a fairyland held up on columns of magic?

Socks, realizing that Henrik's attention was no longer on her worship, dug claws into his knee as she leapt away.

"You were about to ascend a level?" Henrik said, point-edly looking at the gaming screen. It was certainly more than he'd ever volunteered about the world he came from and Gwen didn't want to push him any further.

Chewing over the new information, she turned the game back on and was quickly immersed in her more accessible digital goals.

he days crept closer and closer to the date marked "Thanksgiving" on the house calendar and there was still no news from Robin or Tadra's key.

Both of Henrik's shieldmates had tried repeatedly to scry, but neither of them had ever been skilled enough to cross such a distance. Henrik himself peered into every reflective surface he could find, staring until his eyes crossed, wishing for the magic that had once come so easily to him.

"They've got cellphones in Ecuador, don't they?" Trey said impatiently.

"Pretty sure they have all the modern conveniences," Daniella told Trey. But she also looked worried, and she often watched down the long driveway as if she expected them to suddenly drive up it.

There was a gigantic plucked bird in the refrigerator, thawing in a plastic tub of water. A turkey, Gwen explained, and she showed him a video of a flock of large, foolish-looking birds who made a curious gobbling sound. There were many rituals to be observed for this holiday, apparently, and Daniella and Heather both seemed to spend an inordinate time on their own cellphones appeasing their families about their inability to attend distant gatherings.

Some part of Henrik expected Robin to pop through a portal at any moment the next day.

Surely they were only waiting until the last moment in order to make a dramatic entrance.

Daniella even arranged them a seat on the table, their smaller table draped with a lace handkerchief and placed with a small china tea set. There was certainly enough food to accommodate several extra mouths.

The incomprehensible game of football that Ansel and Heather liked to watch was put on in the game room with the door open so that the cheers and music infused the entire house. Trey and Rez were enraptured by the sport and the mesmerizing commercials.

Henrik was coerced by Daniella and Gwen to assist in the kitchen, where he chopped bright orange potatoes and celery and onions and more familiar white potatoes. Every appliance seemed to be in use: both ovens and every burner on the stove were all being used, and every inch of counter space was filled with the food in progress.

Heather left the television long enough to make a pie, shouting back down the hall every time there was the sound of a score.

There was no meal planned in the day besides the elaborate dinner, something Henrik only realized when Daniella rapped his knuckles for stealing sticks of carrots from the platter she was filling. The scent filling the house did nothing to suppress his growling stomach; as the day went on, it only smelled better and better.

There was a selection of cheeses and a bowl of round crackers that were permitted snacking before the feast.

Heather gushed over a soft pimento cheese full of tiny red peppers. Gwen stuck to safer cubes of mozzarella. Henrik sampled everything he was permitted.

There were pies, and bread, and something called *dressing* that did not look at all like clothing, and a dish that Heather waxed joyfully over called green bean casserole that was covered all over in crispy fried onions. "Mama's would have bacon in it," she pointed out.

There were fresh rolls, and the orange potatoes were covered in dark sugar and soft white marshmallows. There were regular white potatoes as well, smashed smooth, and bowls of potato chips, as if that were not enough kinds of root, and little dishes of olives and fresh vegetables and green salad with bottles of a completely different kind of dressing called "ranch." A jewel-red sauce of a berry called cran came straight from a can, complete with imprints of rings from its vessel.

"That's part of the charm," Daniella insisted, when Ansel protested that he could make a homemade sauce.

And then there was the turkey itself, which Daniella insisted on taking from the oven, straining at the weight of it and beaming proudly. It was a glorious fowl, baked to steaming perfection, covered with a crisp golden skin. It was brought triumphantly to the table, where they were all seated, and Ansel, who had elected himself the carver, paused a moment and looked at Robin's place setting.

Heather bowed her head and gave a short prayer that ended with, "And may we all eat together with our missing friends really soon. Ingeesussname, amen."

Henrik had no idea what *ingeesussname* was, but the ritual was obvious. When her words came to an end, Gwen squeezed his hand. He wasn't even sure when she'd taken it, but she let go then to begin serving food, and they all dug in with gusto.

The turkey was deliciously moist beneath its crackling skin, and when smothered in the odd can-shaped jelly, a terrific treat. It was all rather amazing, and they ate enthusiastically for some time.

Heather talked about things she would have eaten at home. "Bacon," she said. "There would have been bacon in everything. Green bean and bacon casserole. Bacon collard greens. Bacon in the gravy. Bacon crumbles in the salad. Mama even put bacon grease in pecan pie."

Gwen nodded knowingly; the two were from a similar southern area of the land of America, and they often laughed together over the curious things that 'the northerners' did.

"We didn't celebrate American Thanksgiving when I was growing up," she explained as she cleared the last of her mashed potatoes off her plate with a roll. "But we did observe *Chuseok*, which translates to autumn's eve. It's basically the same thing except three days long and a little earlier in the year."

"Did you eat these foods?" Henrik wanted to know, gesturing to the decimated spread.

"No, we ate traditional Korean foods, like *songpyeon*, a stuffed rice cake, and Korean pancakes. Oh, and *yugwa*, which is a kind of fried cookie. We'd exchange gifts. Really *practical* gifts, like toothpaste and coffee."

"My mother used to think socks were a great gift," Heather said sympathetically.

"We should celebrate Chuseok next year," Daniella suggested, and everyone became solemnly quiet as they considered the idea there might not *be* a next year.

"I have no room for pie right now," Heather said too brightly into the silence. "But the second game is coming on. I'll help clear up and load the dishwasher."

Cleaning up seemed as much effort as the preparation had been, but it went swiftly with many hands.

Ansel took charge of repacking the refrigerator. "Nobody cook anything for a week," he warned. "I don't know if the floorboards here are designed to hold up this much weight."

"I don't know if *I'm* meant to hold up this much weight," Gwen groaned.

Henrik carried dishes from the table, trip after trip, and very grimly took down Robin's place setting.

atching him at the cafe a few days later, Gwen could almost believe that Henrik was just his cover story, a perfectly un-magical immigrant from Norway. Trey and Rez had trained him up quite well, and he shyly told Marie just enough made-up details about his fisherman life in the LoFoten Islands. They'd even found him a cable-knit sweater that barely fit over his muscled shoulders. It didn't make him look the tiniest bit less sexy.

Then he tried to explain that tomatoes were not available in Norway, to Marie's confusion, and the others deftly took over the conversation.

Heather was sitting with the three of them, and Daniella was waiting tables across the cafe while Gwen handled the espresso machine.

"It was nice of Trey to import you such a swoon-worthy *friend*," Marie told her as she passed by, bussing the table's dishes. "They sure do grow them large in Scandinavia."

Gwen grinned at her and finished the latte she was making. "You have no idea," she said, thinking about

Henrik as a pigeon-sized gryphon curling up with her cat, and Trey, big enough to fill the garage.

As she delivered the cup to the table across the room, there was a sudden scream from the kitchen.

"Marie!" The entire table of knights rose as one, reaching for weapons that they weren't wearing. Gwen was already scrambling straight over the counter towards the back.

Marie was standing near the open back door, a trash bag still dangling in her hand. Gwen had a glimpse beyond her of a sinuous shadow, bigger than any dour she had ever seen, and before she could get halfway through the kitchen, it had slithered up and into Marie.

Gwen knew what to expect from a dour. Marie would be Marie, but the very worst of her. She would sound and look like Marie, but twisted in anger and hatred and irrational fears. Gwen just had to keep her from harming someone in her fit, and one of the knights would come and purge out the darkness that was tainting her spirit.

But when Marie turned, Gwen sucked in a breath of sharp air, because it wasn't Marie at all, and she wasn't just primed for a fight, she was there to start one.

The bag of trash hurtled towards Gwen with more strength than she even thought that Marie had, and while Gwen was busy dodging it, Marie took up two of the big butcher knives from the block on the counter and charged forward. The trash bag split when it hit the counter, spilling garbage everywhere.

"Hold it, Marie!" Gwen said, spinning out of her way. "Remember that this isn't you! I'm your friend!"

"You're the gryphon's key!" Marie snarled. "We're here to end you, human!"

Then there was a spitting ball of golden feathers screeching like a bird of prey from the dining room door.

Gwen watched one of the knives arc expertly towards the oncoming gryphon with a sinking heart and almost sobbed when Henrik managed to wheel out of the way at the last moment.

"She's got a dour!" Heather said in dismay, and Gwen spared a glance to see the two other keys arranging themselves at the doorway, Daniella drawing in a deep breath and Heather reaching into the air above her. They were blocking the door to the dining room, and Trey and Rez were standing at their side, clearly gauging the space against their magical forms.

"It's more than a dour!" Gwen said, returning her attention to the battle. "It was big, and not just chaotic. She knows about *us!* All of us!"

Marie drew up then, and just as Trey and Rez were advancing down the aisle by the ovens towards her, she suddenly flipped the knives in her hands and placed the blades at her own throat. Everyone froze.

"You know the best part about taking an innocent human host?" someone else's voice asked from her throat. "They're weak and pathetic, but you'd do anything to keep them from harm." She looked towards Heather and smiled too wide. "Even landlords that don't deserve any better."

"Release the human and fight us yourself," Trey snarled. "Or are you a coward?"

Marie laughed, a terrible, un-Marie sound from her twisted face. "So noble," she cackled. "So honorable. And you expect everyone else to be, too." Thin lines of blood appeared at her neck. "I have no interest in exposing myself even to your feeble magic."

Gwen felt sickeningly helpless. She didn't dare press forward; her techniques for disarming were for weapons being used against *her*, not against themselves.

Suddenly, there was a streak like fire, and Henrik was landing on Marie's head.

Surprise made the blades withdraw a hair, and even while Gwen was trying to figure out what she could possibly do with that tiny opportunity, there was a sudden snap, like the world's tiniest transformer blowing, and lightning sizzled around Marie.

If Gwen hadn't been staring at Marie, she probably wouldn't have noticed the expression on her face going briefly slack; whatever Henrik had done, it had separated the *dour-thing* from human for just a moment.

What should she do? What *could* she do? Gwen longed for a pause button so that she could investigate the manual for clues.

But this wasn't a game, and it hadn't come with a manual. Marie was slicing with both knives over her head at Henrik, who tumbled backwards out of her reach.

Trey and Rez had not hesitated like Gwen had, and they were within arms length of Marie now. There wasn't room for either of them to shift, but Daniella was singing and Heather was knitting the air.

"You will release the human!" Trey commanded, and there was something in his voice that made the woman shiver. Rez dashed forward and laid a hand upon her shoulder before she could recover, and there was an unworldly cry of pain and fury as the darkness fell away from Marie's face and shivered back into a dour nothing like the ones that Gwen had seen before.

It was the size of a large dog, undoubtedly bigger and fiercer than Fabio, with eyes like pits to nowhere. Its shape shifted and smeared, as if Gwen had tears filling her eyes. It gave a rusty howl, and flattened into a puddle, slithering out the open door behind it and vanishing down through the slats in the porch.

Marie staggered in place and dropped her knives, looking dazedly around.

Rez let go of her and dashed out the back door in pursuit of the creature.

Henrik landed and shifted, exchanged one guilty, mournful look with Gwen, and followed him.

"Are you okay?" Daniella asked Marie anxiously.

"What happened to the trash?" Marie wanted to know. The waste was spread out over the counter it had hit, trailing onto the ground.

"You must have tripped," Heather said. Trey was already starting to pick it up.

Shaking her head, Marie went to get a new bag. "Huh," was all she said.

The cafe customers were all clustered at the door to the kitchen that Daniella and Heather had kept shut. "What happened?" "Is everyone okay?" "Should we call the police?"

"Everything's fine!" Daniella insisted. "Just an...uh...errant trash bag! We'll get it picked back up and get back to work. Might be a little delay in the food. Nothing to worry about!"

Marie wandered out then, looking much more herself. "What a lot of fuss for nothing," she scolded. "I just dropped a trash bag, will you people get back to your tables?" She had just the right air of sheepishness and impatience to send everyone scurrying back to their seats.

25

*H*enrik and Rez searched beneath the porch, around the back of the cafe, and behind the large metal container that reeked of trash, but the thing was truly gone.

"If I had access to the magic, I could trace it," Henrik said miserably. "I could dowse for danger, and ward our safe places. I could scry, and..."

"Do not blame yourself," Rez said kindly, and he might have drawn him into an embrace, but Henrik didn't want his shieldmate's comfort.

"Who shall I blame, then?" Henrik demanded. "Gwen? A human woman thrust into a role she never wanted, trying to do something none of us know how to do? Robin, for sending us here? Cerad, for his relentless hunt? Tadra, for not being here to stand at our shoulders? I should be able to protect us! I should!" He sank into a crouch. "I should be able to protect *her*."

Rez's hand squeezed his shoulder, tightly, but he said nothing.

Nothing would have helped.

Henrik gathered his wits, shamed by his outburst, and stood again. "We have a new kind of threat to consider," he said gravely, and he stalked back into the cafe.

Gwen was sterilizing the counter, and the look she cast him held no blame.

"We were unable to follow the dour," he reported.

"How was that a *dour*?" Gwen wanted to know. "Dours are little. They don't control people like *that*."

Marie returned then, and she shook her head tolerantly at Henrik.

"Your boyfriend's not supposed to be back here," she reminded Gwen, but she winked at Henrik. It was unnerving how different she was than she'd been such a short time prior.

It was a topic of great interest later, when they were all safely back in the great house of Ansel.

"It did not appear to act as a dour would," Trey said thoughtfully, after they had traded notes about what each of them had witnessed.

"Not the dours I've seen," Daniella said. "It was smarter, not just bigger."

"Superdours," Gwen said wryly, kicking off her shoes. "That's just what we need." She curled her feet underneath herself and cuddled on the couch next to Henrik. Her nearness was some comfort.

"The entity appeared to be controlling the human in full," Rez said thoughtfully.

"It knew who we were," Heather said. "And it k*new* about my landlord in Georgia. Was it a *bleak*? The same bleak, maybe? We stopped that one, but it got away."

"It didn't look like other bleaks," Rez said. "And Marie wasn't a willing vessel like Marcus. It acted like a dour, but was intelligent like a bleak."

Something terrible occurred to Henrik. "Could it be a burned-out false key?"

Beside him, Gwen shuddered and everyone else stared at them.

"Dours are the ashes of magic," he pointed out. "Chaotic and simple. They do not direct, they only sow darkness. This is more like a bleak than a dour, but diminished in power. If a bleak were to take a willing vessel and burn them to nothing, is this not what might result? A dark, bodiless minion which could possess independent direction and purpose, able to slither into a human as a dour can?"

"A reduced bleak," Gwen said wryly.

"A reduction of bleak," Heather giggled.

"A redux of bleak," Daniella added.

Their ladies laughed, clearly near hysterical.

"I like the term *superdour* better," Rez said solemnly.

That only made them break into more peals of helpless laughter.

"Okay, look," Daniella said, rising to her feet. "Henrik's theory is as good as any, but what we should do is try to get a little more information, and stick together. None of us alone was strong enough to knock it out, but six of us were." Henrik thought it was kind of her to count him. "We don't know how many of them there are, or where, but we know they are after us *specifically*, so we should be careful about going out alone. And I also know that if we starve to death, we won't be able to save the world."

"Sorry to break up the war meeting," Ansel said, standing in the doorway to the kitchen with a rectangle of paper in his hands. "I was going to order some takeout, if you guys are as tired of Thanksgiving leftovers as I am."

"Pizza!" Henrik said, but the suggestion immediately reminded him of Robin, still missing. Robin would know better than them what this new menace was, and how to counter it, even diminished as they were here.

"Pizza," Trey agreed mournfully.

"Pizza," Rez chorused with Heather.

"Geez, guys, don't sound so excited about it," Ansel said, but his face suggested that he understood their sadness.

It was the same delivery driver who had delivered their pizzas weeks before at Marie's cafe, and he looked no more amused than he had the previous time. "Veggie, two pepperoni, meat festival, and chicken fiesta, extra spicy." He looked them over skeptically. "Nice house."

"It is Ansel's," Rez pointed out politely as he took the steaming boxes. "He is gracious enough to allow us to live and train here."

"It has a refrigerator," Henrik added.

The delivery lad nodded slowly. "Sure, man."

Ansel signed the receipt. "They're Norwegian," he said apologetically.

The driver scurried away with suspicious quickness.

26

The second hand store was technically open, but as usual, there were no customers, which was just as well, since everyone was coming to pack up the warehouse and minimize the damage that the coming battle would do.

"I don't know how you stay in business," Daniella said, hanging her coat near the door.

"Thanks, nice to see you, too!" Ansel called from the counter. "I'll remind you that the weeks before Christmas are usually my most brisk sales, and that I'm closing early in the year, *for you guys*, so that you can save the world without as much collateral damage this time. Hopefully."

"You're our hero, Ansel," Gwen called. "Maybe they'll write a ballad about your sacrifices." She took off her coat.

"Will it be a rock ballad?" Henrik wanted to know. Gwen had been introducing him to more styles of music. He'd been alarmed by K-Pop, enthralled by jazz, and bored by classical. Queen remained one of his favorite bands.

"It was just a joke," Gwen explained. "I was teasing Ansel."

Henrik looked vaguely disappointed, and since he was standing close enough, bent to give her a kiss that she was perfectly happy to accept.

"Alright," Daniella said commandingly. "Girls, let's start with glassware, since that's the most fragile. The knights can start moving out the furniture. Most of it can go in the storage unit out back. We'll stack the boxes on the furniture. Clothing and the display racks and shelves last."

"I'll leave you to it," Ansel said. "Please label the boxes so that I have some hope of finding things again."

"We will of course unpack for you once the crisis is past," Rez assured him. "This is the least we can do."

"Yes it is," Ansel agreed with a laugh. "Alright, I'm going to close up and call it a year. I'll have dinner ready when you guys realize how much you've bitten off."

"It will take us several days I fear," Trey admitted.

After a few hours, and about a hundred bubble-wrapped glasses and baubles, Gwen was starting to feel like it was going to take them until *Christmas*.

Robin, who was still worryingly missing, had wanted them to start monitoring the warehouse in mid-December, to make sure that Cerad's forces didn't try to punch through the veil unexpectedly while it was thinning but not yet its thinnest.

Henrik felt bad about not being able to scry for Robin, or dowse for Tadra or her key, or do anything useful, and Gwen hated how he took that guilt upon himself instead of putting it on her where it belonged.

The others remained optimistic, frequently reiterating that it had taken external forces to bring their magic to light. They smirked at Henrik and Gwen no less than they

had before, but Gwen cared less now that they were
spending every blissful night together.

"Sorry, we're closed!" Daniella called, when the door
gave a little chime. No one answered, but Gwen continued
to hear commotion in the front. The door chimed again,
and again.

Daniella brushed off her knees as she stood to go talk
to them directly. "Some people can't take a hint," she
sighed.

Then she got to the end of the aisle and screamed
Trey's name at the top of her lungs.

Gwen was rolling to her feet before Daniella could turn
and run back.

"What is it?" she asked in alarm, unconsciously
standing in a fighting stance.

Before Daniella could answer, Gwen saw them.
"Marie?" she said hesitantly, but she already knew that it
wasn't Marie. Not any more than it was Mr. Strickland, or
that guy from the corner market, or the woman who
jogged with her dog down Jefferson street every day at six,
or their pizza delivery driver. They were clearly possessed,
puppets at the hands of the darkness that glared from their
eyes.

There was a press of them, and Gwen wasn't sure
what was the cold of the darkness they carried, what
was the cold swirl of air from the door they'd left open,
and what was the chill of her own despair. They
weren't ready! She hadn't figured out how to unlock
Henrik's energy, and she hadn't thought to bring her
sword.

"Is there a sword in this place?" she asked desperately.
She was going to figure out how to unlock this power
sooner than later, it looked like.

"In costumes, maybe?" Heather suggested.

"Wait, I think there's one behind the counter," Daniella said.

The three of them had retreated, shoulder to shoulder, and the mob of superdour-ridden people was advancing on them, slowly but inexorably. It wasn't quite a zombie shuffle, but it was clearly un-hurried. They were grinning in anticipation.

As badly as Gwen wanted to keep her fellow keys at her side, she stepped forward away from them. "I'm going to need a little space," she warned them, flexing her fingers.

The zombies paused as she stepped to face them. "I don't want to hurt you," she told them. "Okay, I don't want to hurt the humans. So, just let them go, and...uh...I won't have to hurt you?"

Okay, she wasn't great at the negotiating part.

One of them laughed, a man holding a length of chain. Marie was holding two of her biggest butcher knives and the jogger woman had an axe. It looked more like a wood-chopping axe than the kind of battle axe that Henrik used, but Gwen was pretty sure it would hurt if it connected. The delivery boy had a baseball bat.

"You won't harm us," Marie said. "But we have no such qualms about hurting you. Only you stand between this world and glorious victory. If we remove you, we will have favor with the darkness coming. We have new masters now, and new vessels."

Gwen sighed, and took swift inventory of herself as she calmed her breathing. Her shoelaces were tied, her pants were stretchy enough to allow her to kick, and her shirt was not too loose. She wasn't wearing a Do Bohk, but she didn't need the uniform to fight.

She just had to take them down and then the knights could get the dours out of the poor people. It was just...there were a lot of them.

Before she could lose her nerve she gave a loud "Kiyep!" and dropped into a position of attack. "Come get me, you jerks!"

Unfortunately, they accepted her invitation.

27

"*D*aniella!" Trey dropped the end of the couch that he was carrying, leaving Rez and Henrik at the other end to try to keep the piece of furniture from careening off the ramp to the storage unit into the snow. "She is distressed! She is in danger!"

That was reason enough for Rez and Henrik to abandon the couch as well, sprinting back to the warehouse.

Trey shifted as he went through the door, cracking the frame, and Rez was his magnificent stallion self, leaping over Trey's lashing tail.

The only way that Henrik was going to get past them to Gwen was if he shifted, too, so he did, keenly aware of the uselessness of his still-tiny form. He winged his way up, above Trey's great head. From this vantage, he could see a terrible battle spreading out through the warehouse. Gwen was crouched facing a half dozen humans armed with a variety of deadly tools, looking small but not helpless. Daniella and Heather were behind her, and none of them were aware of the other two humans coming down the next aisle to flank them.

Henrik did not have to see their faces to know that they were driven by dark forces. Gwen had called them superdours.

He gave a shriek, wishing for human speech at the least, but he knew that his warning would be understood. He darted through the air and fell upon the two super-dours who were creeping around behind the keys, scratching and snapping his beak at them. One of them he actually landed on, using the magic he could dredge up to snap at their source like he had with Marie.

As it had with Marie, it only lasted a moment before the dour was back in control of the human. If Trey and Rez had followed him, perhaps it would have lasted longer, and Henrik rose into the air to join his shieldmates.

They were working in tandem on the group of ridden humans attacking Gwen, and Henrik chose the human they were nearest. Snap!

Between the three of them, the dour was stripped from the body it was possessing and the human staggered back in confusion from the battle it found itself in.

Gwen was taking on too many of them, Henrik thought in miserable dismay. She was a flow of water, a measure of music, and using her skills to great advantage. When they attacked, she used their strength to throw them down, or to twist them aside. But they had weapons to her bare hands, and there were many more of them. A man swinging a chain caught her in the side and battered her into the shelves that they had been clearing. Books tumbled off swaying shelves onto the fighters.

Daniella and Heather began picking them up and throwing them into the fray, but swiftly realized that their efforts were not helpful and chose to flee—directly into the two ridden humans coming around behind them.

Gwen got back to her feet and Henrik landed on another dour-ridden victim close to Trey and Rez. *Snap!* Henrik could feel the strength drain out of him as the dour's hold released for a moment.

But Trey was already leaping over the battle, his big wings spread as he surged to protect Daniella and Heather, and the moment of opportunity was gone. The man lifted his weapon, a bent pipe, and struck Henrik off his head before he could dodge.

Tumbling helplessly, Henrik saw Gwen darting between all of the aggressors. At first he thought that she was coming to help him and wished he could warn her back. But she did not pause, dashing past him to the front counter and vaulting over it. As Henrik righted himself, he saw her purpose. Behind it on the wall—clever key!—a sword was hanging.

Several of the ridden people peeled off to follow her and Henrik was appalled to see that the one they'd managed to free was re-infested, the darkness oozing into them like a rotting stench once more. Trey and Rez were fighting together by their keys.

Gwen leapt back over the counter with a warcry, using the flat of the sword to slap back the weapons menacing her. But she was hampered by her desire not to harm the hosts, and the damage she dealt was too minor to stop them. One of them raised a wooden club at her, and she struck it aside with her blade. They were too many, and though she twisted and fought with grace and skill, Henrik knew she must be tiring.

He dodged a whirling chain and banked just in time to see Gwen's sword slice the air and embed in the wood of the counter, thoroughly stuck. One of the ridden humans was swiping at him with a racket of some kind and he had to tilt to avoid the blow, losing sight of her in the fray.

28

*T*he sword...was stuck. It was wedged hard in the side of the wooden counter and Gwen could only yank on it desperately and weep in frustration.

She could feel the magic, like her eyes were closed but she could see light through her eyelids. But none of her fighting seemed to do even the tiniest bit of good to her control of it or her ability to throw the power to Henrik the way Heather and Daniella described.

And Henrik was slowing and tiring, darting less and less quickly to attack as Trey and Rez did the heavy lifting. Henrik who would fight his heart out while she helplessly let him down.

This was the moment that everything was supposed to click into place, wasn't it? They were outnumbered and outmaneuvered and they were losing. When would her blade light on fire or whatever crazy thing needed to happen to make the magic *work*? There were no moments more desperate than this!

The sword refused to budge, and Gwen leaned back

and tried to wiggle it loose, but she simply wasn't strong enough.

She wasn't strong enough, she wasn't fast enough, she wasn't *ever* going to be.

She would fail as a key like she'd failed every other expectation for her life.

Even her fighting wasn't good enough. The only other things she was good at were drinking coffee and playing video games.

The sword, though it wasn't moving from the counter where it was lodged, flexed in her hands, like a sticky joystick.

A...joystick.

Gwen remembered sitting on the couch next to Henrik, showing him the parts of the controller, reminding him that he didn't have to move his whole body in order to activate the functions. "Just your fingers," she'd said, thinking entirely too hard about his fingers at the time. "Little motions. Subtle. You won't win with strength."

She stared out over the battlefield of the warehouse, at the handful of possessed people they were trying not to hurt...and not be killed by. Trey and Rez had to defend Heather and Daniella, as well as try to separate the superdours from their victims. They were divided and disorganized, barely fast enough to react to each new threat. And every time one of the humans was freed, the superdour crept right back into their shaken host.

She longed for a pause button...she could see too well how their resources were poorly distributed, how badly they needed to regroup and re-evaluate their strengths. If Henrik's shock attack could stun them long enough, if she could coordinate Trey's flame and give Rez the time to apply his magic...all at once?

It was all about timing. Like a video game.

Gwen released the hilt of her useless sword and stepped back. A man was roaring towards her, his features full of ill-intent and his hands full of baseball bat. Gwen didn't try to run or dodge or lift an arm to defend herself, but centered herself and pictured a controller in her hands. A new controller, for a completely unknown game with no user manual.

All she had to do was logic herself through how it might work and watch for clues. If she was playing a game, she'd pause for a moment, to familiarize herself with the menus and commands.

And to pause the game, she just had to…

Gwen closed her eyes and imagined a pause button under her thumb, hyper aware of the swing of the bat coming at her, that she wasn't leaving herself enough time to dodge, not with mere human reflexes.

She braced for the blow…and it didn't come.

Her eyes flew open, to a frozen tableau of their losing battle.

The man before her had his bat raised to strike, but had been caught out of time before he could.

Gwen threw her head back and laughed in release and surprise. She had paused the game. She had *paused* it.

And if she could pause it, what else could she do?

She touched the man with the bat cautiously, ready to dodge out of the way at the slightest hint of motion. He was immovable, and when Gwen tried experimentally to adjust his arm, she heard an error noise, clear as day. *Blat.*

She remembered Robin trying to explain magic. Magic was outside of logic and understanding, operating within rules that human brains simply didn't comprehend. Daniella's song, Heather's knitting, even the way that each of them saw a slightly different image of the fable, it was their mind filling in blanks, supplying information that they understood at a subconscious level in a way that they would respond to. It was even the way they each saw Robin with vastly different kinds of wings, to explain how they flew. Gwen's perception of magic was put into a platform that she understood. When she couldn't do a thing, she got a response that her mind would interpret, in her case a video game noise.

Blat, indeed.

It was a lot to take in, and for a moment, Gwen stood there and poked the unfortunate man with the bat. She couldn't manipulate him directly, she decided, so what *could* she do? Could she somehow release him from the darkness riding him, in this weird out-of-step moment?

Blat, blat, blat…

Gwen finally left him in peace and circled the room. She could touch things, but not move them. She could not adjust any of the player positions, and she could not arm anyone. She frowned, assessing the scene from a tactical point of view, no longer simply reacting to a nearby threat, but looking out over the whole thing as a complete game board.

There weren't actually that many of the superdours. They were just persistent, and her friends were handicapped by their desire not to actually harm any of the hosts. It took all three of the knights to release a host from their evil rider, and it was only a temporary respite. Their current tactic was just keeping their enemy at bay; if they wanted to actually win, they had to group together and actively protect the hosts they freed.

They had to change their strategy. Gwen could feel the pause button under her thumb as she wandered the room. The moment she released it, everything would jolt forward again, with the same momentum as before. She had to *change* that momentum, somehow.

In a game, she'd be able to direct her avatars. In games where she controlled a lot of people, she could assign them tasks, set them a queue of commands to work through. How would she do that here?

Stop thinking in a box, Gwen scolded herself. *How would you do it in a game?* She closed her eyes, thinking about how to queue up commands. There would be a menu…

When she opened her eyes, she almost laughed again. Over every head was a status bar, her friends edged in green, her enemies in red. All she had to do was select a player and add to their actions list…or target the correct enemies, as if they were weapons she was controlling.

Blat.

No, she didn't think she'd be able to manipulate the ridden humans.

But when she tried with Daniella, the same thing happened. *Blat.*

Free will, perhaps? What if she couldn't affect anything at *all?*

Gwen frowned. Okay, so what if it was a multi-player game? Maybe she couldn't affect the other players, but she could…send them a text, coordinate things behind the screen? Could she suggest something? She stood in front of Daniella and concentrated. There was a man swinging a heavy club at her from behind. The first thing she'd have Daniella do was…*duck.*

A sudden chatbox appeared above Daniella's head, floating ridiculously in space over her. *Duck!* it said.

It's just my brain trying to make sense of what the magic is doing, Gwen reminded herself. *It's not really as literal as this.*

She circled the room, adding chatboxes to all of her friends with the first things she wanted them to do. She paused at Henrik, caught in mid-air as he dodged back from a swinging chain. His energy bars were dangerously low, with warning arrows.

How do I fix that?

Was there a backup power source she could apply? A healing potion? A bonus energy booster?

Blat. Blat. Blat.

Nope. Gwen looked up, suddenly curious to see whether she had her own energy bar.

It wasn't over her, it was over the space where she'd been standing, but sure enough, she was fully charged. And she wasn't the critical one in this battle, the knights were the ones who had the ability to remove the superdours and defeat their enemies. She had to figure a way to transfer that energy from her, to Henrik.

Ding.

Her power bar went down, Henrik's rose.

Ding, ding, ding, ding! How much did she dare transfer? If she emptied herself, did it mean *actual* death? Was there a spare life tucked away in this crazy magic game? She had to assume that death was final, and there wasn't a save point she could go back to.

She emptied her power bar down to a single red tick with a dire warning arrow, filling Henrik's to overfull, and called it good.

Then she circled the room again, plotting strategy.

Finally, chatboxes filled with directives, power siphoned to where it needed to be, Gwen felt like she was as ready as she was going to be. Heart in her throat, she closed her eyes and envisioned thumbing off the pause button.

Blat.

She cracked an eyelid.

Had she trapped herself in some kind of timeless void by accident? She glanced up for her own power bar for some kind of clue...and remembered that it wasn't above her.

Oh, crap. Her power bar was back where her body had been, directly in the path of a bat that she wasn't going to have time to avoid, once time had meaning again.

Reluctantly, she put herself in back where she'd been and envisioned her thumb lifting slowly off the pause button.

This was going to hurt.

29

*H*enrik felt a moment of cold certainty settle in his throat when he caught a glimpse of Gwen getting the sword stuck in the counter.

They'd been caught by surprise, and were badly hampered by their desire not to hurt the vessels of the evil they were fighting. He could feel his energy waning, he was barely more than a distraction in this battle, while Trey and Rez could muster some effectiveness at least.

Then, very suddenly, several things happened at once.

All of his energy returned, not only as it had been, but unexpectedly *more*, like he was suddenly a creek filled with rushing water. He was power, he was—

Bank left! Now!

Gwen's voice was loud in his ear, commanding and urgent.

Henrik obeyed out of instinct, spreading his wings wider than they had yet been and yanking himself left just as a chain sizzled through the air where he'd been.

Focus, Henrik! Fly wide and get back around to Trey and Rez. It takes three of you at once to keep the superdours from the victims and they ooze back in if you leave them too long, you have to get them herded together and do them all at once. I've got everything in place, you just have to follow the plan!

Her voice in his head assured him that Gwen must be safe, though he could not see her, so Henrik streaked across the warehouse to where Trey and Rez were both shaking their heads in surprise and amazement.

They roared in greeting as he completed his sweep and landed between them.

He was his full, glorious size once again. Gwen had done it! His amazing, clever key.

Instructions, in Gwen's steady, sensible voice unrolled in his inner ear, and he could see that Trey and Rez were receiving the same instructions.

In unison, they scattered to the corners of the room, confusing and disorienting their enemy. The keys were in motion as well, giving up their positions of defense to draw them all together in the center of the cleared space. Evenly spaced around them, at Gwen's crisp orders, the knights attacked in unison. Trey lay down a spray of his fire, too thin to be effective on its own, but Rez bowed his head and gave a jolt of his blue healing magic. The two together were enough to drive the superdours from their hosts, but Henrik knew that as soon as the pressure they were exerting was released, the humans would be possessed once again. Henrik reached down into the leylines that were vibrating all around them and cast a ward spell.

To his pleasure, the magic answered, flowing effort-lessly out of him over the humans, forming a glowing dome that sizzled in his magic-sight.

The shadow forms of the ill-named superdours shiv-ered back, gathering in the corners of the room.

Now, they just had to shrivel them into nothing with their combined powers. Henrik stepped forward, reveling in the feeling of his powerful body and full size as his shieldmates flanked him.

He almost didn't notice the crackle of a portal at first.

"Robin!" Daniella cried. "Robin is back!"

But it wasn't Robin, and the bleak who stepped through was not friendly. It had a black sword, the mirror of the one that had menaced Socks.

For a moment of horror, Henrik thought that it was a portal to their home world, that the invasion was already in place. How did their calendar work? Had they grossly misjudged the strength of the veil? But the bleak was alone, and although the portal remained open behind it, snapping with energy, no one else came through it. It looked like a green jungle behind it.

It was only a small respite.

The bleak said, in its voice of oil and despair, "You may think this is a victory because you saved a few humans, but I assure you it is not. We already have the broken crown, and our time is drawing near. Come! Come my children!"

It turned as if to lead the dours back through the portal.

Like water, the cornered superdours rose onto their not-quite-feet and slithered and oozed around the edges of the room. Henrik could feel the energy of the whole room change and cool, and he felt hot fury rise up in his chest in response.

He was not going to leave the bleak to escape unscathed with its evil army. Not while he had a drop of power in him. He reared up and spread his wings. He didn't have Gwen's words in his head any longer, but he could still feel the power that she had given him.

Before Trey or Rez could react, he was charging forward.

There wasn't room for actual flight, but a powerful leap

closed the space between them and Henrik was pouncing and weaving a spell and shrieking all at once.

The superdours shivered and the bleak looked up at Henrik's attack in surprise and dismay before it shivered into smoke—just as Henrik's counterspell closed the portal, slicing it—and the sword it was holding—in half.

The superdours howled and broke down, demoralized, as Trey hit half of them with his flame and Rez stampeded straight into the fray, blue light flickering from his striking hooves. Henrik, reaching into his remaining power reserves, spun another spell like a web of glowing strands that settled over the shades and trapped them together as he squeezed his will onto them.

They screamed and slithered, but his net was too tight to escape, and with his shieldmates at his side, their own magic concentrated on the captured creatures, they slowly dissolved each of them into a puff of smoke and a pile of ash.

Henrik did not note the silence in the room until Trey touched him with human hands, drawing him back from the constricted web of ash and memories.

"Are they gone for good?" Gwen asked behind him, "or did they just dissolve in that way they do?"

"They are gone," Trey said confidently.

Henrik turned and shifted in one move to find that Gwen was leaning heavily between Daniella and Heather. There was blood on the side of her face.

"My key!" he said in agony. "Are you hurt?"

"No more than you'd expect from a baseball bat to the head," Gwen said flippantly. "I was able to distract him with voices in his head questioning his manhood, so it wasn't as solid a hit as it could have been."

Henrik swept her up into his arms as gently as he could

manage and clung to her desperately. "My key," he murmured into her short hair.

"I wasn't sure any of it would work," she said dazedly. "But it was all I could do."

"Should we take her to a doctor?" Daniella asked anxiously.

"Excuse me?"

Henrik had managed to forget about the warded humans. He hastily dropped the ward.

"Gas leak!" Heather said at once, as loud as she could. "There's a gas leak! That's why you're all feeling so woozy and disoriented! You should get into the fresh air!"

Trey and Rez began herding the humans out into the winter night.

"What am I doing here?"

"Is it snowing?"

"Where are we?"

"What happened to the shop?"

"Oh geez," Gwen groaned. "We're going to have to explain this to Ansel again."

*a*nsel took the news of another battle in his second hand shop with much more grace than Gwen would have managed. Most of the glassware that they had laboriously wrapped for storage had been broken in the battle, and many of the shelves had been smashed. "You can help me with the insurance paperwork," he said with resignation. "And buy me a case of beer. And someone else can make dinner tonight. And also, we should open a bottle of wine."

Fabio made slow nervous laps and Vesta leapt up into an unclaimed chair, shivering anxiously. Socks made one foray into the room, decided it was too crowded for her tastes, and left with her tail up.

The broken tip of the sword that had remained behind on their side of the portal had drained of its black color, but Henrik took no chances with it, laying a sparkling yellow light over it that faded away to nothing. He explained that it was a ward and also started to cast a protection on the whole house, but then stopped in confusion. "It's already warded," he said in surprise.

"Robin?" Trey guessed.

"Yes," Henrik said, his eyes closed. "I think so. It is a circle, and it did not include the corner of the garage where the sword was resting. Probably it would have never activated if it had been hung with the others."

Gwen was sitting on the living room couch wrapped in an afghan, barely able to hear their conversation. When she tried to struggle out of the blanket that Henrik had wrapped her in, she found it unexpectedly complicated. Henrik returned with a frown while she was trying to find an end.

"I'm not hurt that bad," she said, still struggling for freedom. "Rez said I was fine and used his sparkly unicorn magic. Look, symmetrical pupils! He said so!"

Henrik kissed between her eyes and tucked the blanket around her more firmly.

"You gave me all of your power," he chided her. "You should never have done that."

"I had no idea what I was doing," Gwen said with a tired chuckle. The couch deflected as Henrik sat down and she sagged armlessly into his side. "I think I can do a better job next time. I wasn't sure how much it would take, and I didn't want to skimp. If I hadn't gotten clobbered in the head, I think that I'd have been able to recharge and feed the power to you more continuously like the others do."

"It was a worthy sally," Trey said admiringly. "Your directions were quite clear and turned the tide of the battle swiftly."

"You were an admirable director," Rez agreed, laying one hand over his chest and bowing his head.

Gwen squirmed, as much as she could with the blanket pinning her. "It wasn't that much."

"How did you do it?" Daniella wanted to know, bringing in wineglasses on a tray. "None for you," she chided Gwen, who pouted and subsided into her cocoon. "We have sparkling cider for the head injury."

"Rez miracled me," Gwen protested. "Symmetrical pupils!" Her head didn't exactly throb any more, but she still felt a headache lurking behind her eyes, so she didn't argue much. "You know how I thought the only thing I was good at was karate? Well, I neglected the fact that I'm a pretty kick-ass game player. I didn't figure that was *worth* anything, you know? But once I started to think about that, I could...sort of imagine everything around me in gaming terms and it all fell into place. Help, I'm stuck."

Henrik obligingly unwrapped her and propped her up so she could take her glass of cider.

"It was very impressive," Daniella said, passing out the other glasses.

"And a little unnerving," Heather admitted. "It was like being...texted in the brain."

"I liked having your words inside my head," Henrik said. Gwen wondered if he didn't sound a little smoldery and she started to take a sip of her cider.

"No, no, we have to toast!" Daniella said.

"Toast!" Trey agreed.

"What does this have to do with crisp bread?" Henrik wanted to know.

"A toast is a salute," Rez explained. "We lift our drink and celebrate a win, respect a comrade, or express gratitude."

"The bleak said it wasn't a victory," Gwen remembered abruptly. "It said that they already had the broken crown."

She felt terrible as soon as she said it and the mood of the room abruptly dampened.

"What does that mean?" Heather asked softly.

Trey shook his head. "I don't know. The crown fell long before we came into our power. Robin told us that the crown had ruled our world in peace and harmony for untold years before Cerad betrayed the kingdom and broke it, but he never told us exactly what happened to it."

Gwen unconsciously snuggled closer to Henrik's side and saw Daniella and Heather both draw closer to their knights. Ansel, standing by himself, stared into his wineglass.

"To the broken crown," Rez suggested, raising his drink.

"To Gwen, who really came through as a key!" Heather said, eager to brighten the room.

"To Henrik," Trey added. "Our shieldmate."

"To all of us," Henrik protested, mimicking their toast.

"To insurance," Ansel said wryly.

"To Robin," Rez said mournfully, and everyone took a long sip of their drinks and thought about the empty places that the fable usually filled.

"To Tadra, and her key, may we meet them soon," Daniella said belatedly, and they drank to that, too.

They finished their wine and talked quietly about nothing while Heather made a quick dinner of spaghetti and garlic toast.

The meal was cheerful and relieved. Henrik agreed that garlic toast was a marvelous improvement on regular toast.

Afterwards, everyone crowded into the kitchen to help with the cleaning. When Gwen tried to get up and help, Henrik insisted that she sit, so she remained at the table in the dining room, listening to the quiet chatter from the kitchen. Fabio came in and made a circle of the room, but swiftly decided that Gwen had nothing worth begging for.

Robin's little chair and personal table were still set up on top of the dining room table. It was already December, somehow, and the veil between worlds would already be thinning. But they'd gotten rid of the superdours, and it would take time for the bleak to make a new army of them.

Henrik came back into the dining room and knelt at her feet. "My Gwen," he said adoringly.

Gwen looked down at his soft curls and broad shoulders and pondered at how weird and how wonderful her life was. "I love you, Henrik," she said quietly, and when he looked up at her with his golden eyes filled with affection and joy, she felt like her heart might overflow.

Her life wasn't at all what she'd feared when she first agreed to follow Robin through the portal; she wasn't trapped with someone she was forced to feel things for. She was head over heels for this man because they were perfect for each other. Like two magnets. Like destiny. "You want to head upstairs a little early?" she suggested. "I'm pretty tired…"

Mischief flashed in Henrik's eyes. "I understand that you aren't supposed to go to sleep with a head injury," he said leadingly.

"I wasn't thinking about sleep," Gwen whispered.

Henrik rose to his feet and swept Gwen into his arms in one smooth motion. Gwen clung to him and laughed. "I can walk!" she protested. "I didn't get hit in the legs!"

Fabio and Vesta, drawn by the commotion, galloped into the dining room and danced around Henrik's feet as he carried her out to the living room and up the stairs. Gwen giggled and sighed into his embrace.

Socks was sleeping on Gwen's bed, and she stood up with a hiss of disgust when Henrik lowered Gwen onto the bed and then bent to join her, making the bed dip.

Gwen reached up and pulled him down over her, loving how solid his arms felt under her hands, the feeling of his knees pinning her hips, the fall of his hair…

Socks yowled in displeasure and leapt over them to escape, pausing at the door to lick her shoulder in their general direction and remind them that the door was shut, with her on the wrong side of it.

Henrik obediently rose to open the door and release her in return for an ungrateful mrrrrt. Gwen took that opportunity to shuck off her clothing, and Henrik was stripping off his jeans as he returned to the bed.

He gathered her back into his arms while she was tugging his t-shirt up over his head, and he sucked in a breath when she dragged her nails down his back and pulled him down with her, kissing everything she could reach with her mouth.

His own mouth was like fire on her skin, at her neck, the base of her throat, down between her breasts while she flung her head back and clawed the bed. His hands were equally busy, cupping each breast in turn and caressing the nipples until they were hard little pebbles under his thumbs, stroking the curve where her waist met her hip.

He kissed down to her belly, and she buried her fingers in his soft hair while he licked and nibbled, lower and lower, finally laying his lips at her waiting, wet entrance.

Gwen made a wordless keen of pleasure and anticipation, writhing at his touch, and when he began kissing his way back up her body, she felt like she was a fever pitch.

"Yes, yes, please," she begged as he crawled his way to straddling her, his iron-hard cock dragging along her leg until it was pressed where his lips had been.

"My love, my *key*," he said, adjusting them both in little ways until he could enter her, in one long, smooth stroke and Gwen thought that maybe she'd been hit in the head a little harder than she knew, because her world exploded into stars.

They made slow, deliberate love, pursuing every peak

of pleasure and riding every tiny release as they worked to a fever pitch of bliss.

"I love you!" Gwen cried, when she felt like she could take no more, and she was wrong, because Henrik's passionate response lifted her somewhere new, and afterwards it was a long, long while before either of them was able to move again.

"Thank you," she murmured in his ear, not even sure what she was thanking him for. For loving her? For trusting her even when she hadn't trusted herself? For being everything she hadn't known she wanted? For turning her body into a limp puddle of euphoria?

"Your problem," he answered sincerely, and he could not understand why she collapsed into hysterical laughter.

EPILOGUE

"Tell me more about Christmas," Henrik said eagerly, clipping the lights into place over the garage. He slid down the ladder and moved it, while Gwen held the tangle of the cord and handed it up to him to hang once he'd climbed back up. "Heather explained some of the history, but said that it was very different in different places. Tell me about your Christmas."

"Well, people do celebrate it in a lot of different ways," Gwen told him. "Hold on, this is tangled." She deftly unwound the knots and passed up more of the green strands, broken periodically by tiny colored lamps.

"My family wasn't as into gifts as commercials will have you believe most Americans are," she continued, standing aside as Henrik came back down the ladder. "But we did a dinner a lot like Thanksgiving, and we exchange cards with family. We watch Christmas movies, and there are usually candles."

"Trey showed me the Little Drummer Boy," Henrik said. "It was very sad. And Rudolph, the Poor Reindeer. And Charles Gray."

"Charlie Brown?" Gwen guessed.

"Yes," Henrik agreed.

"Did they tell you about Santa Claus?"

"The large red-dressed man who brings gifts? Yes, but I had such questions!" Henrik installed the last of the lights and backed down the ladder. "How does this man make it so far all over the world in the allotted time? Does he have the ability to pause time such as you do? I thought that people of your world did not use magic."

"My mother always said that Santa Claus was more like an idea. That he's meant to represent the best and most unselfish of what we could be. She used to say that anyone could make miracles if they had the right heart."

"You have the right heart," Henrik said, bending to kiss her as he stepped off the last run.

"Aren't you the sweetest thing," Gwen said warmly. They were both wearing puffy coats, and hugging Gwen was like hugging her through a pillow.

"What gift would you like?" he asked her, after he set her back down on her feet.

"You don't have to give me a gift," she protested. "I know you don't have any money."

Henrik had already been warned that Gwen would make this pretense. "I could make you something," he offered.

"You don't have to make something," she insisted, exactly as Ansel had told him she would. But she looked pleased at the idea, like she had when he had praised her beauty.

"Perhaps I could cook you a meal," Henrik suggested. "Something that features toast. Or I could craft you something. Ansel has many tools."

"Ask Ansel first," Gwen reminded him. "Let's see what these lights look like now."

She went to the corner of the garage and plugged in the string of lights.

It was only just beginning to grow dark, and the colored illuminations were bright and cheerful against the dimness.

"It is delightful," he said joyously.

"I'm freezing," Gwen said. "Don't fae knights ever get cold?"

"Rez says that marshmallows can be put in hot chocolate," Henrik said hopefully. His shieldmates kept going on about how marvelous *toasted* marshmallows were, but he had not had the opportunity to enjoy them yet. He had not been impressed with the plain marshmallows, but knowing what toasting did to bread, he was eager to try them.

They went in the garage door, putting the ladder back in the corner and stomping the snow off of their boots. Henrik gave a glance to the weapons rack as they went to the house, opening the door carefully to keep the eager dogs back. The tip of the bleak's black sword had been hung with the other blades, including its warded full-sized twin. He often looked to reassure himself that it was still a dull steel color.

Other than the wound up dogs, the air in the living room was unexpectedly subdued.

"What's wrong?" Gwen asked at once, unwinding the scarf from her neck.

Henrik was still shrugging his coat off when Heather said grimly, "We found Tadra."

"That's great!" Gwen said. Then, as she took in the solemn faces of everyone around her, "That's great, right?"

"I got a call from the ornament shop where I used to work," Heather explained. "My bosses have been keeping an eye out, and someone finally brought a glass phoenix in."

She paused and looked around at Trey and Rez, who both looked gutted. "They were hoping that they could get it repaired, because it had been dropped...and broken into pieces."

A NOTE FROM ZOE CHANT

Thank you so much for buying my book! I hope you enjoyed Gwen and Henrik's story (at last!). I would love to know what you thought—you can leave a review at Amazon or Goodreads—I read every one, and they help other readers find me, too!

You can also email me at zoechantebooks@gmail.com. I really enjoy hearing from my readers and if you find any typos, feel free to email them to me directly so I can fix them.

If you'd like to be emailed when I release my next book, please visit my webpage, zoechant.com, to be added to my mailing list. You can also find me on Facebook and are invited to join my VIP Reader's Group, where I do sneak previews and cover reveals!

Read on for information about some of my other series, and a sneak preview of a world just north of familiar…

~Zoe Chant

The cover of Gryphon of Glass was designed by Ellen Million: ellenmillion.com. The ornament on the cover was commissioned specifically for this book from A Touch of Glass. Their webpage is: glass4gifts.com

Carina Andresen surged to her feet, sweeping her camp chair out from under her as a make-shift weapon.

Wolf! her brain hammered at her. *Wolf!* She was going to become an Alaska tourist statistic and get eaten by a wolf on her second week in the kingdom.

Logic slowly caught up with her panic.

The animal across the campfire from her was smaller and *doggier* than a wolf, and it was only a moment before Carina could get her breath and heartbeat back under control and recognize that it was well-groomed, shyly eyeing her sizzling hot dog, and wagging its tail.

Alaska probably had stray dogs, too; she wasn't *that* far from civilization.

"Hi there, sweetie," Carina said, her voice still unnaturally high as she put her chair back on its legs. "Does that smell good? Want a bit of hot dog?" Carina turned the hot dog in the flame and waggled it suggestively.

The non-edible dog sped up his tail and when Carina broke off a piece of the meat and dropped it beside her, he crept around the fire and slurped it eagerly up off the ground.

The second bite he took gently from her fingers, and by the second hot dog she dared to pet him.

Within about thirty minutes and five hot dogs, he was leaning on her and letting her scratch his ears and neck as he wagged his tail and groaned in delight.

"Oh, you're just a dear," Carina said. "I bet someone's missing you." He was a husky mix, Carina guessed; he was tall and strong, with a long, thick coat of dark gray fur and white feet. His ears were upright, and his tail was long and feathered. He didn't have a collar, but he was clearly friendly. "You want some water?"

The dog licked his lips as if he had understood, and Carina carefully stood so she didn't frighten him.

But he seemed to be past any shyness now, and he followed Carina to her van trustingly, tail waving happily. He drank the offered water from a frying pan, and then tried to give Carina a kiss dripping with slobber.

"You probably already have a name," Carina said, laughingly trying to escape the wet tongue. "But I'm going to call you Shadow for now." She had a grubby towel hanging from her clothesline and used it to dry off his face. They played a gentle game of tug-of-war, testing each other's strength and manners.

Shadow seemed to approve of his new name and gave her a canine grin once she'd won the towel back from him.

"Alright, Shadow, let's go collect some more firewood."

The area was rich with downed wood to harvest, and with the assistance of a folding hand saw, Carina was able to find several heaping armloads of solid, dry wood, enough to keep a cheerful fire going for a few days if she was frugal. It was comforting to have Shadow around for the task; she wasn't quite as nervous about the noises she heard, and he was a happy distraction from her own brain.

He frolicked with her, and found a stick three times his own length to drag around possessively.

"So helpful!" Carina laughed at him, as he knocked over an empty pot and swiped her across the knees so that she nearly fell.

When she sat down beside the crackling fire in her low camp chair, Shadow abandoned his prize stick and crowded close to lay his head on her knee. Carina petted him absently.

"Someone's looking for you, you big softy," she said regretfully. She would have to try to reunite the dog with his owner but, for now, it was nice having a companion around the camp.

Of all the things she expected when she went running for the wilderness, she had never guessed that the silence would be the worst. She had been camping plenty, but it was always *with* someone. Since their parents had died, that someone was usually her sister, June, but sometimes it was a friend or a roommate. She was used to having someone to point out birds and animals to, someone to share chores with, stretch out tarps with. When it was just her, the spaces seemed vaster, the wind bit harder, and even the birds were less cheerful.

"You probably don't care about the birds that would make my life list," she told Shadow mournfully.

Shadow wagged his tail in a rustle of leaves.

She didn't have her life list anymore to add to anyway. Everything had been left behind: her phone, her computer, her identity. Her entire life was on hold. She had the van to live in, some supplies and a small nest egg to start from, so she ought to be able to stay out of sight long enough to regroup and…she didn't know what to do from here. Find a journalist willing to take her story and clear her name?

To fill the quiet, and to help ignore the ache in her chest, she read aloud from the brochure on Alaska that she had been given at the border station. She'd found it that evening while she was emptying the glovebox to take stock of supplies, and Shadow seemed as good a listener as any.

"Like many modern monarchies, Alaska has an elected council of officials who do most of the day to day rulings of this vast, rich land. The royal family is steeped in tradition and mystery, and holds many veto powers, as well as acting as ambassadors to other countries. Known as the Dragon King, the Alaskan sovereign is a reserved figure who rarely appears in public. Margaret, the Queen of Alaska, died twelve years ago, leaving behind six sons." There was a photo, with boys ranging from about seven to maybe twenty-five. Two of the middle children were identical. One of the twins was wearing a hockey jersey and grinning, the other wore glasses and looked annoyed. The oldest—or at least the tallest—was frowning seriously at the others. The only blonde of the bunch was one of the middle boys, who was looking intently at the camera. The youngest looked painfully bored. They all had tongue-twisting names of more syllables than Carina wanted to try pronouncing.

Carina thought it was an interesting photo. The tension between the oldest two was palpable, and the they were all dressed surprisingly casually. She didn't follow royal gossip much beyond scanning headlines at grocery store checkouts, but Alaska never seemed to make waves; they were rarely involved in dramas and scandals.

Shadow raised his head and cocked his head at some imagined noise in the forest.

"That's a lot of siblings," Carina observed, ruffling his ears. She felt so much safer having him beside her. "Just one sister was more than enough for me." She didn't want to admit how much she missed that sister right now.

Shadow returned his head to her knee. "Alaska is a member of the Small Kingdoms Alliance, an exclusive collective of independent monarchies scattered throughout the world. Although Alaska has large amounts of land, they qualify for membership because of their small population."

Carina turned the brochure over. "There are hot springs about fifty miles north of Fairbanks! I hope to make it there." *Before* she ran out of cash. It looked expensive. Maybe she could get work there...she'd heard that it wasn't hard to find under-the-table jobs in this country.

Shadow suddenly leapt to his feet, barking at something crashing through the woods behind them and Carina nearly tipped over backwards in her camp chair trying to stand up.

She expected to find a moose, or possibly a bear, and she was already picking up the chair to use as a flimsy defense against a charging wild animal.

But it was only a man stepping out of the woods, in an official dark blue uniform emblazoned with the eight gold stars of Alaska.

For a moment, terror every bit as keen as the panic that had gripped her at the first sight of Shadow washed over her. They'd found her.

"You're trespassing on royal land and I'm going to have to ask you to leave," he said.

Then she realized with relief that it wasn't a police officer. He was only a park ranger.

◆

...or was he? Discover love and adventure in a wonderful alternate Alaska with camping and dogs and magic. Reluctant royalty and relentless enemies! Pick up The Dragon Prince of Alaska *today!*

Shifting Sands Resort

Writing as Zoe Chant

* Hot, strong, protective shifter heroes...who aren't jerks.
* Capable, complicated shifter heroines...who aren't doormats.
* Fresh new plots, not recycled stories, with unique magic and fantasy worldbuilding.
* ALL THE FEELS.
* Diverse leads: queer, disabled, multicultural, not all the same shape, the same color, or the same animal.
* A gorgeous tropical setting that you'll desperately wish you could visit.
* A complete 10 book series with a thrilling conclusion.

A luxury shifters-only resort on an island full of secrets…Shifting Sands Resort is the series you didn't know you were waiting for. Hot, hilarious, and heartwarming, each book is an electrifying standalone with a satisfying happy ever after...but they all tie together into an epic magical mystery that will leave you flying through the books.

Start the series with TROPICAL TIGER SPY, in which Tony Lukin uncovers the first of many mysteries and finds the love of his life.

Green Valley Shifters

Writing as Zoe Chant

The books of Green Valley Shifters are set in a small town with single dads, spinsters, and shifters. Each one is a sizzling standalone with heart-warming, found-family humor, hunky shifters, and sweet second chances.

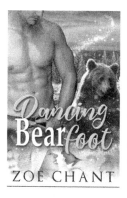

In DANCING BEARFOOT, bear shifter, billionaire, and single dad Lee is only looking for a quiet place to raise his daughter Clara when he moves to the sleepy town of Green Valley. He never believed in soulmates, but when he meets Clara's new teacher, he knows at once that he's met the woman who can make his new house a home.

In THE TIGER NEXT DOOR, it's bad enough that Shaun doesn't know the first thing about being a father—now suddenly he's the father of an unpredictable shifter child. Abandoned by his mother, all that Trevor has ever asked for is love and stability, and tiger shifter Shaun is determined to give that to him at any cost. Even if it means denying that the hot next door neighbor is his destined mate.

In DANDELION SEASON, Tawny Summers has her retirement all planned out: catch up on her books, work on her garden, and teach piano lessons to children in the tiny town of Green Valley. Her plan doesn't include a gorgeous city billionaire with piercing silver eyes who is determined to upend her quiet life and frighten her cats.

In BEARLY TOGETHER, lion shifter and lawyer Shelley Powell has to face her fear of children and all her many insecurities, including clinical anxiety, to be with her mate, bear shifter Dean James. All of sudden, instead of negotiating contracts, she's figuring her way around an active seven-year-old, a drooling dog, and an ex-wife who is everything she isn't.

Coming in 2020: BROKEN LYNX. She's a firefighter. He's…a waitress? Devon, programmer and lynx shifter, takes whatever odd jobs he can around raising his little sister after their parents die. Into his over-complicated life comes Jamie, a firefighter from Alaska, who manages to set his entire life on fire…

SHAPE SHIFTERS

Writing as Elva Birch

From fated mates to fairy tales, from the cold depths of space to hot wildfires in Alaska, Elva Birch spins entrancing tales of love and *transformation*.

These seven stories range from flash fiction to novellas, at various levels of heat, with a variety of pairings (lesbian, transgender, and menage). Some have been previously published in anthologies, some under other names, and several are new and exclusive to this collection.

Includes: Better Half, The Dazzling Finister, Balance, Breakup, Fire Control, The Neighbors Might Talk, and Leashed.

Made in the USA
Middletown, DE
30 January 2021